Past Legends

The Camelot Immortals

A. F. Stewart

Past Legends
A. F. Stewart

Editing by C. Mitchell Editing

Cover design by A. F. Stewart
Original artwork licensed by Adobe Stock Photos

ISBN: 978-1-9990659-7-3

Thanks to my niece Jaime, who helped with the research
and my beta readers for their wonderful insights.

The Camelot Immortals Books

Eternal Myths

Past Legends

Gathering Hallows

Broken Branch

Wayward Prophecy

Contents

Prologue

How It Began

Once upon a myth, or legend, or tall tale, or whatever you want to call it, there existed a wondrous place called Camelot. Full of knights and wizards, magic and quests, a beautiful land of enchantment, fair maidens and ruled by a just king.

Not quite.

Camelot was more akin to a Dark Ages lunatic asylum. I should know, I lived there.

Let me introduce myself. I'm Nimue. I'm a witch and I've been alive for fifteen hundred years, give or take a few decades. These days I live in Cumbria, England, in the Lake

District, but a long time ago, I lived in the aforementioned Camelot, that mysterious land of magic and legend. Also a place with no running water, no modern medicine, and where basic hygiene could be iffy. Warriors in leather jerkins and dented helms roamed its dusty roads, not knights in armour, and usually held a drink in one hand while the other groped a woman's—well you get the idea.

I never meant to get involved, with either Camelot or magic, but one day a handsome stranger walked into my father's tavern.

Merlin, the grand wizard of Camelot.

I should have stayed in the tavern.

Merlin, among other things, was a liar, a psycho, and a wanker. When he held the temptation of magic in front of me, he conveniently forgot to mention the consequences. Like the small issue of immortality. Or his control issues.

What can I say? When you're in love you do stupid things.

And what's done is done. I moved on, adapted, and reinvented myself over the centuries. To keep busy in these modern times, I run an off and on holiday let and an online crafts business. It's not much different from other lives I've led, with the exception of all this technology. Of course, things haven't always gone smoothly; recently there was that mess with Excalibur and then Elaine going after the Grail. Everything worked itself out, though, with a little help.

And I even got a bit of revenge. A while back, I turned Merlin into a tree, and now he's a wonderful addition to my garden...

Chapter One

Visitors

"Tell me again. What are the fundamentals of magic?" I put cucumber on the last of the sandwiches while quizzing Martin on his lessons. He was proving to be a clever wizard, but somewhat inattentive to the basics.

He snitched a cucumber slice. "Magic is an underlying energy that flows through all the dimensions. It runs like unseen rivers, surrounding us, manifesting itself through ley lines, power sites, and between the netherworlds."

"Excellent. What are the three systems of use?" I placed the finished sandwiches on the tray. "I can't believe Elaine never taught you this. It's Magic 101."

"I know this." Martin grinned. "The first system

is minor magic, where we use spell words to draw energy from the matrix. That's how a wizard throws energy bolts or fireballs or levitates, and a few other things. Major magic is for all the rest; it needs prepared spells or potions. There are also subsystems of major magic such as earth magic or blood magic that utilize certain types of ingredients. And the third one is Ascendency, which confused me."

"Don't worry about Ascendancy. It's a dangerous and complicated transformation to gain power, and how gods are created. Most wizards avoid it. You should pay attention to ascendant channelling, though. Anytime you harness any external energy source, that's what you're doing."

"Oh, Elaine did that. We trekked off to a ley line and she mumbled some words to boost her magic." He grunted. "It worked at first, but when she tried to steal the Grail it all fizzled out."

"Not surprised. She doesn't have enough skill to channel that wild magic properly." I took the milk out of the fridge and poured some into the creamer, filling the small pitcher. "Now, what is the difference between immortal wizards and other magic users?" Behind me the kettle whistled, and I poured hot water into the teapot to steep the tea.

"Um," Martin frowned. "We live longer?"

I sighed. If he only paid as much attention to his lessons as he did his recipe books. "No, we go through the binding ritual. It's what separates the true practitioners from the spell dabblers. It's why we're immortal and they just get a healthy longevity."

"Oh, yeah. Elaine did that to me." He shivered. "It hurt."

"She always was heavy-handed with her magic. Her father's like that too. The Fisher King isn't one for a gentle touch." Poor Martin. Sucked into our world without much of a clue, other than his grandmother's spellbook and the rantings of a crazy witch. Family legacies can be a pain. The least I could do was apprentice the unlucky sod after I had dealt with Elaine.

"We'll take a break for now, and eat. Take that tray to the garden, would you? The one with the food. It would be a shame to waste this lovely summer weather. The nippy autumn air will be here before you know it."

"Certainly." Martin picked up the tray of sandwiches and cake, while I turned to prepare another with the cups and teapot.

"Granny!"

His declaration, as much as the rattle of crockery, caused me to whirl about, dread souring my stomach. She stood in the doorway, dressed in a green frock, her highlighted brunette tresses cut in a stylish, short bob.

"Iseult." My voice wavered, dreading bad news.

"I go by Izzy these days, but yes, it's me." She shifted her gaze. "Hello, Martin."

"You look just like your picture." His hands trembled with more rattling of plates. "Except for the hair. And the new clothes."

Iseult smiled, and for a moment I had absurd hope.

Maybe she stopped by to visit her grandson?

The figure lurking behind her, dripping water on my floor tile, crushed that wish.

I nodded in her direction. "Hello, Viv."

Vivienne, the Lady of the Lake, stared at me with a crestfallen expression. "Oh, Nimue!" she wailed with the decibels of a banshee. "It's gone! The lake entrance to the netherworld is gone!"

Fuck.

All hope of a happy family reunion flew out the window.

I walked around the kitchen island and placed a hand on Martin's shoulder, who was still gaping at Iseult. "Why don't you finish the tea and make some additional sandwiches? I think we three ladies need to talk in private for a bit. You can visit with your grandmother later."

Martin nodded, handed me his tray, and hurried to the counter where he busied himself rearranging the tea cups.

I turned back to the two women. "We can have tea in the garden." I brushed past my guests carrying the sandwich tray. They followed, Iseult keeping pace with me, while Vivienne tagged along behind.

"I was surprised to hear you'd taken in Martin as an apprentice." Iseult's voice was as soft and melodic as I remembered.

"Not much choice. He got his hands on your spellbook. Couldn't leave him on his own without training."

"I heard about that too, although Galahad was a bit fuzzy on the details. He got mixed up with Elaine for some reason?"

"Something like that, yeah."

She plucked at her skirt before asking, "Is he any good, as a wizard?"

I shrugged, as much as the tray allowed. "He's talented, but he needs to work on his focus." We continued on into the garden. I put the tray on the wrought iron table and pulled over a third chair.

"You two sit down and help yourself to some tea. I'll be back in a minute."

I nipped off to the loo where I grabbed a folded towel. I returned to my company and tossed Viv the towel. She flashed me a grateful smile while sopping up the water clinging to her, careful not to drip any onto her cake plate balanced precariously on the table edge.

I piled two sandwich triangles and a piece of seed cake onto a plate and settled into my favourite chair. I took a bite of bread and cucumber and nodded at Iseult, who nodded back as we both avoided the issue.

After a few moments of this, the silence broken only by Vivienne's grunts and rustling, Iseult spoke.

"I found Morgawse." She fidgeted, with a rueful expression of apology. "At least briefly. Tucked away in a magical stasis, in a remote netherworld."

My fingers tightened their grip on my plate. *Shit. She's not here to get nosy about who put her there, I hope. That could get awkward.*

I tugged at my shirt, shifting in my seat. "Well, that explains things, I suppose. At least she won't make trouble there."

Iseult ducked her head and mumbled, just loud enough for me to hear, "She's not there anymore. Someone freed her."

"What?" At that instant, I could have spit but settled for a few curses. "Damnation! Bloody hell! She escaped? How the hell…" And then the rest of what she said filtered in past my anger. "What do you mean, freed? What happened?" I shoved my plate on the table and leaned forward, glaring.

Iseult shrank back in her chair, words tumbling out of her mouth, "I didn't do it. I was in the wrong place at the right time. It was my bad luck to run across her when I was looking for a permanent place to hide. Somewhere away from… them."

My anger eased a bit. "Mark and Tristan harassing you again?"

She nodded. "Tristan is still being a pest. Mark's been less forceful lately, although he has tried to message me. I'm tired of dealing with their obsession, though, and I thought maybe I could lose them in a netherworld." She squirmed in her chair. "I picked the wrong one."

"Damn right you did!" Vivienne's wail returned, albeit less damp. "Why did you go poking about in there? Look what's happened!"

A shiver scattered across my skin. "Spit and bother. What the bloody hell did happen?"

"Calamity and trouble that's what!" Vivienne shrieked loud enough for the garden birds to take flight. "All because Iseult had to go prying about in a netherworld. Nothing good ever comes from that!"

"Vivienne, I keep telling you it's not my fault! I didn't do anything! I stumbled on Morgawse. I was defending myself!"

"What about the netherworlds closing? What about that? You were the catalyst! That's your fault! Yes, your fault!"

"Oh, for pity's sake! I keep telling you that it's likely just temporary! A side effect. You'll be back to your soggy self in no time!"

"Why you—"

"Be quiet! The pair of you." I snapped my words like lightning and roared like thunder. "Vivienne, Iseult, stop the bloody bickering. Tell me what in damnation is going on, and tell me now!"

Their two mouths clamped shut, and they both had the sense to look chastised. At least to me. They still shot resentful glances at each other.

I took a breath. "Somebody had better spill in the next few seconds or else." I gave them both my best death glare.

Iseult set her plate down with a clatter and brushed the hair back from her eyes. "I told you I went into a netherworld and stumbled on the one containing Morgawse. But she wasn't alone, or to be more precise, someone else had found her before I did."

I clenched my fists. "Someone else? Who?"

"I don't know. A dark, shadowy, sinister type. Definitely male, though." Iseult shrugged as if such things occurred every day. Though come to think, maybe they did with us.

"After that, things got messy," Iseult continued. "This

wizard was abducting Morgawse when I interrupted and I got attacked for my trouble. I defended myself against his magic and managed to survive, but he escaped with Morgawse. That's what caused the other problem." She shot another daggered look at Vivienne. "There were some residual effects that may have muddled access to the netherworlds."

"Oh. Well, if they're only residual effects." I let my scorn drip a river between us. "Damnation, Iseult! This is serious! Messing with the netherworld can have long-term consequences. And, oh yes, Morgawse was abducted!"

Vivienne smirked and stuck out her tongue.

"Don't gloat, Viv. It isn't becoming." Sometimes I wondered if I was the only sane resident of Camelot.

"Can I say something?" We turned our heads at Martin's voice. He ducked his head and cleared his throat as he set down the tea tray he was carrying.

"Yes?" I tried to sound calm, but it came out more curmudgeonly. I poured the tea to hide my annoyance.

"Well, um, I," Martin hemmed and hawed before spitting out, "If the netherworld entrances closed, how did you get out, Granny?"

Iseult's mouth flopped open like a flounder, and I stifled a snicker. She shot Martin a dour look.

He ducked his head sheepishly. "Sorry, Granny."

"Don't be. It's a valid question. How did you get out, Iseult?"

"I—I—shit!" Iseult had the decency to blush. "It wasn't like he kept fighting me. He chucked some spell at me, and I deflected it. After that failed attempt, he fled with an unconscious Morgawse tossed over his shoulder like a side of beef. So I chased him, but he portalled out." She shrugged again. "I hitched a ride on his portal. I think my presence may have overloaded the spell."

I put my teacup down to avoid throwing it at her. I took a breath. "Of course it did, you ninny! You know how delicate the fabric of reality is, especially between this world and a netherworld! It was an idiot thing to do!"

"And what was I supposed to do!" She flung the retort like a child flings a hated pudding. "I didn't have time to make my own! He was kidnapping Morgawse! Morgawse! Arguably the second most powerful witch in all creation!"

"So your solution was to destabilize the entire

netherworld!" Vivienne shrieked in displeasure. "I knew it was your fault! You've always been careless!"

"That's enough, Viv!" My patience shattered. "It wasn't the best decision, but she's right about one thing. The effect of overloading a portal isn't likely permanent. You'll have your link back soon." I shot her a look. "So simmer down. I need to ask Iseult some questions."

I turned on Iseult like a predator and she responded with the look of a cornered animal. "It wasn't my fault. I tried to stop him!"

"Who?"

"I truly don't know. But he—he was… unsettling. There's no other word for it. The essence of his magic radiated like a summer's heat." She closed her eyes for an infinitesimal second. When she opened them, I saw her unease. She exhaled, rather loudly. "His energy felt unnerving."

I leaned back in my chair. "Interesting. Do you think he was something conjured? A wraith, perhaps?"

"No." She drew the word out slowly. "He was alive… powerful. Yet, his magic felt different. Almost raw, elemental."

A shiver chased up my spine, trailed by a shudder. Spit

and bells, I hoped it wasn't one of *those* creatures. Elementals are decidedly tricky and unpredictable.

"Could you describe him?" Martin piped up again. "I mean, well enough for me to draw?"

I grinned. Sometimes the boy used his brain. "Like a sketch artist on one of those crime dramas?"

"Exactly."

"Yes," Iseult's soft voice interjected. "I think I could do that."

"Great." Martin lit up like the stars. "I'll get my sketch pad." He made ready to toddle off.

I frowned. "Wait." Martin stopped mid-turn. "Take Iseult with you, into the parlour. There's good light and more privacy. I need to ring Morgan about this anyway. She'll want to know about her sister." I rose, glancing at Vivienne. "Wait here, and enjoy some tea. We'll be back soon enough."

The three of us left the garden as Viv settled back in her chair with her cuppa. I bee-lined for the telephone in the front hall. As I picked up the receiver I caught Iseult looking at me.

"A landline? You lose your mobile?"

I suppressed a smile. "Don't have a mobile, just a landline in the kitchen, and here in the front hallway."

Shock radiated over her face. "No mobile! Are you mad?"

"No. Why would I want a device where people could bother me on a constant basis? I get enough trouble tossed my way as it is. Now off to the parlour, you two." I waved my hand and shooed them away, and buzzed Morgan's number.

The phone rang a couple of times at the other end before Morgan's voice answered with a brisk, "Hello."

"Morgan, it's me, Nimue. Can you talk? It's about your sister. Morgawse was abducted from the netherworld and may be in trouble. Big trouble."

Silence greeted me from the phone. Then, "I can't talk now, but I'll ring you later." The sound of a disconnected line hit my ear and I hung up the receiver. I wondered if I could count on Morgan for this one, or if the bad blood between the sisters would get in the way. At any rate, I had informed her. The rest was up to Morgan.

I wandered back out to the garden and sat down. I topped up my cup with more tea, wishing it was mead.

Vivienne wriggled in her chair and then cleared her throat.

"Spit it out, Viv." I gave her a look and drank some tea.

"How did she take the news?" Vivienne asked in her best stage whisper. "Is Morgan going to help? The way things are between them, I wouldn't blame her for staying away."

"I don't know what she's going to do. She said she couldn't talk and hung up on me." I ran a finger along the rim of my cup. "She did promise to ring me later, so there's that."

I watched Vivienne relax, settling back into her chair. "Good. Not an outright rejection. You must convince her. We'll need her."

I looked at Vivienne sharply. "Is that a premonition? Is there something you're not telling me?"

"No." The word came out of her mouth slowly, as if she was trying to convince both of us. "Not exactly. Just a feeling. Like this is a beginning, and…" She stopped mid-sentence, then added, "Just convince her to help, Nimue. However you can." Vivienne stared into her half-empty cup of tea, saying nothing more.

I cursed inwardly and silently, wishing all the more I had mead instead of tea. I drained my cup and poured another, nursing the drink and the silence between Vivienne and myself. I stared at a scuffed spot on the table leg as we waited for Iseult and Martin to return.

Mid-sip of my just-poured third cup of tea, Martin and Iseult walked back into the garden. I looked up. "You two done?"

Iseult nodded. "Yes, we managed to come up with a good likeness."

"Here, let me see." I put my cup down and held out my hand for the drawing. Martin passed me the pad. One glance and I nearly jumped out of my chair.

"Hell, it can't be!" I tossed the sketch on a nearby empty chair, a shiver running along my skin. "Iseult, did you notice the back of his right hand? Did he have a red mark, a crescent shape near the thumb?"

She frowned, crinkling her brow. "There was some mark. Maybe a crescent shape. It's hard to remember. He was tossing a spell at me when I saw it."

"Shit!" I slammed my hand down on the table, jigging my cup with a clatter and a slosh of tea. "It can't be him!"

"Who?" Iseult's voice trembled. "Who is he?"

"Michel de Nostradame. You know him better as Nostradamus." I nearly choked on the name. "If that's who you saw, then we have major trouble, worse than you can imagine. If he's gone rogue..." I shivered at the thought.

"Isn't he that psychic French bloke?" Martin chimed in on the conversation, confusion in his eyes. "The one with all the prophecies? I thought he was dead. How can he be dangerous?"

I nodded. "That's him, and he's still alive. He faked his death way back when and joined the ranks of immortals. He's also extremely powerful — which makes him a threat. Could be he's unstable as well. Those visions of his sometimes twist him sideways." I sighed, remembering the last days I had spent with him. "When I knew him he was a formidable wizard, though not yet immortal. He loved magic and knowledge, but had some odd ideas." I sipped some tea to drown my conflicting emotions.

"After his ritual, he feigned his death and pursued the study of magic, wandering all over Europe. Last I heard though, he headed off to one of the outer nether-realms in 1707, looking for the ghost of John Dee." I glanced up at three incredulous faces. "Don't underestimate him, he was one of the most powerful sorcerers I knew. He rivalled Merlin." Behind me, his shrub rustled its leaves and I knew I had touched a nerve. I almost chuckled.

"You knew, *know*, Nostradamus?" Iseult asked, her tone a mix of disbelief and awe.

As I nodded, Vivienne added with some snark, "Intimately, if I remember. Our Nimue gets around."

I shot her an annoyed look. "Don't start, Viv. Your past isn't all purity, either. I remember you mooning over Wordsworth for years. Not that he ever gave you the time of day."

She opened her mouth to retort, then closed it, her face blushing. I turned back to Iseult. "But if this is Nostradamus, I've no clue what he's doing, abducting Morgawse. When I knew him he wasn't exactly a man of action. He was all about knowledge, learning the craft, finding new spell books."

"You'd know all about that, wouldn't you?" Vivienne chimed in again with more snark. "Seeing how you liberated some of his books when you left him." I turned to see her smirking at me. "I wonder if he remembers you fondly."

I glared, about to snap at her, when I noticed a glint of silver tucked under the cushion of her chair. It looked like… "Did you find my flask? Have you been drinking?"

Vivienne pouted. "I needed to fortify my nerves. I added a little mead to my tea."

I reached out my arm. "Hand it over."

She dug beneath the cushions and drew out the silver flask, placing it in the palm of my hand. I unscrewed the cap and took a long swig. Iseult gaped and Martin tried to hide a smile. I shrugged. "What? Viv had the right idea. A little fortifying is good."

I extended the flask in a gesture of sharing. Iseult shook her head, a touch of disgust on her face. I glanced over at Martin. He raised a hand, only to quickly lower it at a withering look from his grandmother. I shrugged again and set the flask on the table. Vivienne eyed it, but she didn't make a move.

Iseult tapped her foot in rhythmic impatience. "If you're done indulging, can we—"

A flash of light in the sky interrupted her, and sparks snapped over our heads to ping against the side of my cottage.

I snarled, ready for an attack, but magic slithered along the outside wall and a message appeared in glowing energy.

They seek the lost power that once lay in the tomb. Stop them.

"Bloody shit!" Martin yelled, and I turned in time to see him blush under his grandmother's disapproving look. I glanced at Vivienne who had paled, and then stared back at the message.

I took a breath, unease and fear chasing up my spine. "This can't be good."

Chapter Two

Messages and Memories

I moved forward to take a closer look at the magic. The words shimmered in gold, edged in a touch of blue; a glamour mixed with something I couldn't quite recognize, but which felt familiar. I reached out a hand to get a better sense of the power and the message faded away.

"Damn," I murmured. "Looks like there's another player in the game and they want to remain anonymous." I turned back to the others, seeing confusion as the prevalent expression on their faces.

Iseult exclaimed, "What is going on? What have I gotten involved in?"

Before I could answer, Vivienne stiffened. In a

strange, deep voice, words tumbled out of her mouth, her head snapped back with a jerk, and her eyes rolled in their sockets, turning white.

"It begins. The path of Camelot always led here."

Vivienne shook for a few seconds, then slumped forward. She took a few deep breaths and grabbed the flask off the table.

She gulped mead while I asked, "Your netherworld connection is back then, I take it?"

Vivienne nodded.

I gave her a smile, hoping it was comforting, and returned my attention to Iseult. She stared at Vivienne. Behind her, Martin shifted his feet, his face anxious.

"Been a while since you saw Viv in action, hasn't it?" I asked.

Iseult nodded, repeating, "What is going on?" Her voice sounded tired and bewildered.

I sympathized. Iseult had been away too long. Or maybe I was used to all the weird. I said softly, "What Viv's prattling on about, I have no idea, but I think it best to table that for now."

I shot Viv a look and she nodded, swigging more mead. "As for the disappearing message, my guess is that someone is trying to help in a roundabout way. Who, I don't know." I paused, thinking back. "It did feel familiar, though, so maybe a friend."

"Then why the subterfuge?" Martin piped up. "Why not just say it clear?"

I shrugged. "The world of magic is funny sometimes." I glanced back over at Vivienne, her words rolling around in my head. "There are rules and things you can't interfere with. The cryptic message may have been all they could send."

"Okay. I get that." Martin pursed his lips, furrowing his brow exactly like his grandmother. "Then what does it mean? Lost powers and tombs?"

"I don't know." Irritation crept in my tone and I took a breath to calm myself. "Could be anything. Lost magical tombs aren't exactly uncommon."

Martin still seemed puzzled. "But wouldn't it have to do with Camelot somehow? I mean the message referred to Morgawse and the prophecy guy, right? With '*Stop them*' and all. So, it must have to do with you lot. Otherwise why take

Morgawse? Do you guys have any tomb or—"

"Shit!" I interrupted Martin, who yelped in surprise, and startled Iseult, who jumped. Vivienne almost dropped the flask, before taking another drink. "Shit!"

I groaned. "Martin's right. There is a burial place associated with Camelot. They're going to Arthur's tomb!"

"Arthur's tomb?" Iseult's voice trembled with fear. "No, no, no! He's after the Grail! With Morgawse!" She reached over and grabbed my arm, her fingers clutching me in a desperate grip. "She can command it, you know she can. We have to go now before it's too late."

I pried Iseult's hand off my arm, rubbing the place she had gripped. "Relax. You're probably right, but the Grail's long gone from the Tor. You missed all the fun last year, but I tucked that artifact away where no one can find it." The tension and anxiety faded out of Iseult's body. Spitefully, I added, "That's how I met Martin."

Iseult whirled on her grandson in anger. "That's how you got mixed up in magic? Trying for the Grail?" Her words came out almost a snarl and Martin cringed, backing away a few steps.

He stammered, "I didn't know. I didn't even know about Arthur's tomb. She made it sound like it would be a good thing, and I thought it wasn't really, you know, real. In the beginning. And then she threatened me, and she was crazy. I didn't mean to cause trouble." The last words came out as a pitiful whine and Iseult lessened her accusing glare.

I stepped into the conversation to rescue Martin. "He screwed up to be sure, but it turns out it was a good thing. The Grail's safe."

Iseult took a breath and begrudgingly said, "I suppose." But she aimed one last glare at her cowering grandson.

I ignored the drama and continued. "But if Nostradamus is after the Grail, it might be why he took Morgawse. He'd need one of us to access the tomb." I frowned. "Strange he'd pick her, though."

I moved to the table and poured another cup of tea, prying my flask away from Vivienne long enough to spike it with mead. "At least we know where to go for some answers. Whoever sent the message pointed us in the right direction. With some luck, we can intercept Nostradamus at Glastonbury and stop this mess from escalating. Maybe talk some sense into him or at least find out what he's up to."

"He's probably already there by now," Iseult argued. "Chances are he knows the Grail's missing and has gone looking for it."

"Maybe not. He needs Morgawse, remember? It will take time to bring her out of the stasis spell, and she won't be in any condition to work magic for a while."

Iseult tilted her head. "That would depend on the spell, wouldn't it? Unless you know something the rest of us don't?"

"Of course not," I lied, "but Morgawse is powerful. Stands to reason a spell keeping her under would be equally as powerful."

Iseult looked at me with skepticism. "So now what? We head to Glastonbury and start hunting the passageways of Arthur's tomb? Or lay in wait with some sort of trap?" She scoffed and snorted.

"I don't appreciate the tone or the attitude," I said quietly, putting my cup down. "You came to me with this. You dropped this mess at my doorstep." I added a touch of menace to my words as I continued. "And you're going to help clean it up whether you want to or not." I moved forward until we were eye to eye. "Any more objections?"

Iseult swallowed, frowned, but shook her head. "Glastonbury it is, then."

"Good. Now that's settled, we'll need—" A swoosh of sound and the tell-tale sense of a magic portal grabbed my attention. "We have unexpected visitors! Be alert!" I rushed from the garden into the house, followed by the other three. I prepared a welcoming spell in my head, guaranteed to knock any unwelcome presence on their heels when the door chime rang. I stopped.

Behind me, Martin asked, "Do enemies often ring the doorbell?"

"No, they don't." I marched forward, unlocked the bolt and swung open the front door. Morgan's grim face stared back at me.

"What's going on with my sister?"

I WATCHED Morgan sit in silence after I'd briefly relayed everything that we knew. She stared at the toes of her absurdly expensive shoes, her mouth drawn tight and her fingers clenched around the arms of her chair. I had shooed the others off to the kitchen, so we could have some privacy, and watched as I waited for her to react to it all. It finally came in the form of a quiet whisper.

"She'll help him. Whatever mad scheme or power grab that's playing out she'll be part of it."

I nodded. "It's not your fault. What she does."

Morgan looked up. "Isn't it? I'm the one that put her there. The concealment wards and safeguards weren't enough. Nostradamus still located her."

"That's not all on you. You had help with those safeguards. I thought they'd be enough as well." I sat back and rubbed my temples. "Neither of us counted on a crazy, magic-hungry psychic messing with her prison." I put my hand on Morgan's arm, trying to reassure her.

"That's true." Morgan tapped her fingers against the chair arm. "This was unexpected." She looked at me with a quirk on her lips. "Though with you as a friend…" She tilted her head and added, "Do all your old flames end up slightly psycho?"

I shrugged. "It happens. The good news is we still

have time to stop her, stop them both. Even Nostradamus isn't going to easily break that stasis spell we wove. It could take him days, even weeks. We need to get to Glastonbury and head them off."

Morgan squared her shoulders and shook off my hand. "That's why I'm here. To put Morgawse back where she belongs."

Inwardly, I sighed. I needed Morgan focused on preventing whatever Nostradamus was scheming but the look on her face told me her priority would be her sister. I knew it would be useless to argue.

"We'll stop her." I nodded, in what I hoped was a reassuring manner, despite my misgivings. I would have to work with what I had; a distracted Morgan was better than nothing.

Morgan shifted in her chair, folding her arms. "Do you have a plan? Other than traipsing off to Glastonbury and hoping for the best?"

"The spells we used against Morgawse last time should still be effective. You do remember them?" She nodded. "Good. I've also got a few tricks that may be useful against Nostradamus if it comes to that. I'd like to try to reason with him if only to find out what he's up to with this manoeuvring."

Morgan raised an eyebrow. "Provided he'll listen. I thought you two parted on unfriendly terms."

"Not unfriendly. Uneasy would be a better word. We differed in opinion on certain issues and he was miffed I wouldn't return some of his books. He's not the sort to hold grudges, though." I paused for a moment. "I hope. But nothing seems right about this. The man I knew, Michel, wasn't one for a powerplay." Memories of a strange but fascinating man flitted through my mind. "Perhaps the years as the great Nostradamus went to his head, I don't know."

I lapsed into silence, which Morgan broke with an abrupt change of subject. "And how do we find them? Once we reach Glastonbury?"

I stuffed down the memories and replied, "Hopefully, they'll come to us and walk right into our trap. That's the plan, at any rate."

She nodded in approval. "What about the others?"

"Iseult's agreed to go with us, so we'll have her magic. Viv's no good in a fight, but she's agreed to investigate the origins of the mysterious message and any other ripples in the ether. Martin's going to help her. He's not ready for this type of skirmish."

"So just the three of us?" Morgan flashed a wry, crooked smile. "We've had worse odds. How soon before we leave?"

"I have a few things to gather. Fifteen minutes, if you're ready? We'll leave from the garden."

"Good. That will give me time to change." She hefted the holdall she had brought with her and rose from the chair. "If we're trekking through Arthur's tomb, I'm definitely wearing comfortable shoes and slacks."

She gave me a cheeky salute before heading off to the loo. I made my way to my pantry store cupboards popping into the kitchen on the way. I nodded to Iseult.

"Morgan's in. We'll be leaving in fifteen minutes. Meet us in the garden." I didn't wait for an answer, heading off to gather supplies. I sorted through my stores and packed what I needed in a satchel. I went out to the garden to find Iseult and Morgan waiting. I noticed Morgan had exchanged her fancy shoes for hiking boots and her power suit for casual slacks and a polo shirt, yet she still managed to look stylish. Iseult, on the other hand, looked as if she wanted to vomit and was twisting a lock of her hair around her finger rather obsessively.

I took a deep breath, and let it out slowly, walking past them with a quick, "Follow me."

I led them to the edge of the garden, to a particular stone tucked away in the corner. "I set this up when I first moved here, so I could keep an eye on Arthur if need be. I haven't used it in years, but it should get us to where we want to go."

I reached into my satchel and took out a small bottle of greenish liquid. I unstoppered the cork and poured the contents over the stone. I stepped back and waited, trying not to hold my breath. For a few moments nothing happened, but then the stone began to glow in an amber colour.

It's working.

Then charcoal-coloured energy erupted from the stone in a cascade of sparks and I jumped back in shock. "What the bloody hell?" The sparks sizzled for a few minutes and then died away. The stone continued to glow.

"Is that supposed to happen?" Morgan asked. She stepped back.

To my right, Iseult whined, "Is that thing even safe?"

I frowned. "Something's not right." Then, as I took a step forward, light radiated out and upward from the rock forming a tall, shimmering archway. It hummed and pulsed as the connection between realms solidified until it finally showed the entrance to Arthur's tomb under Glastonbury Tor.

Now it's working properly? What the hell happened? I hesitated, wondering if we should… *No. No time to suss it out now. That will have to wait.*

I took a breath and turned back to the other two. "Just step through, ladies. Next stop, Glastonbury and the burial place of King Arthur." In my confusion, I babbled glibly, but neither woman said a thing as they walked gingerly through the portal. I followed them and the magic passageway sealed shut behind us.

Chapter Three

Arthur's Tomb

I blinked a few times after I arrived, the light from the portal making me see spots. As my eyes adjusted to the dim light of the inter-dimensional netherworld beneath the Tor, I saw Iseult and Morgan standing in front of me. Ahead of us was the doorway to Arthur's Tomb. A shiver ran across my skin. I hadn't been here since the 1900s and those weren't good memories.

I walked forward along the passage—past the other two women who seemed reluctant to move—to the sealed arched entryway. I ran my hand along the stone vault; it tingled under my touch. I studied the grain of the oak door and the familiar protection symbols etched into the wood.

"I remember when we created this place." My whisper shattered the silence. "At the time it seemed like the end of everything. Yet here we are."

With an intake of breath, I moved my hand over the door sensing for a disturbance. I discerned nothing but long past echoes. "I don't think they've arrived yet. It doesn't feel like anyone has entered." Footsteps thumped behind me and the other two moved closer.

I placed my fingers over the locking symbol in the center of the doorway and its magic, Merlin's magic, tingled under my fingers. I shivered; so much had changed since the day we sealed this place. I pressed against the wood and a slight hum sounded.

I whispered the words, "*Camelot am byth.*"

The wood vibrated and the ground trembled slightly. With a loud click and an echo, the door swung open. I walked into the tomb. Morgan and Iseult followed.

Energy snaked across the walls, and sconces burst into magical flame; green spectral torches that illuminated the shadowed room in flickering light. The room was empty except for the far end of the chamber where a golden sarcophagus rested. I stared. I couldn't help myself.

Arthur.

A vision of his rugged, laughing face raced up from the buried depths of my thoughts. I let it dance there for a few moments, basking in the rose-coloured remembrance of past days. Then I turned away. It still hurt. Even after all this time.

I'm sorry, my friend, for how things ended.

I shook off my reverie and walked back to the resealed entrance. While the others watched in undisguised curiosity, I took a pouch from my satchel and sprinkled a grey powder in front of the door.

As I tucked the powder back in my bag, I explained, "An early warning system, so we'll know when they arrive."

Then I brushed past my friends and moved towards the left-hand corridor that led from the chamber, motioning to the others to follow.

"If we're right, and they're after the Grail, then they'll head straight to the old chamber where it used to be kept."

I walked briskly into the new corridor and down the magic-hewn passageway, the thwack of footsteps trailing behind me. Within a few minutes, we arrived in the Grail chamber. The stone dais where it once resided was shattered and its spell of protection as broken as the chunks of rock.

"It got a bit destructive in its escape, didn't it?" Morgan's amusement reverberated around the room.

"It appears so. At least it's safe."

"Are you sure?" Iseult's trembling voice joined the conversation. "What if those two slip this trap and track it down?"

"Doubt it would do them any good," Morgan answered before I could explain. "The Black Knight makes a fierce guard dog. No wizard or witch can best him in a fight."

"The Black Knight?" Iseult's mouth dropped open. "How did you—no, don't answer that, I don't want to know." She took a deep breath and exhaled loudly. "I just want to concentrate on this. What do you need me to do?"

I reached into my satchel and withdrew two small vials, handing one to Iseult and the other to Morgan. "Power enhancements. These will temporarily boost your magic, so you can try to recapture Morgawse while I deal with Mich—Nostradamus. The warning system will be the signal to drink the potion. It won't take but a few seconds to kick in." I paused for a breath and then continued, "We need to separate them. Attack Morgawse in the corridor and hopefully Nostradamus will come straight to me alone."

"Makes sense, I suppose." Morgan tossed in reluctant support. "Divide and conquer."

"What if he helps her? Doesn't go for the Grail room?" Iseult voiced her concerns.

"Unlikely. Michel is nothing if not single-minded, and I can't imagine Morgawse is anything more than a means to his end. But if he does stay and fight, I'll attack from the rear and join you."

"All right," Iseult relented. "It's a reasonable plan. I truly hope he does what you think he will, though. I don't want to deal with his magic again. It wasn't pleasant at all."

I repressed a grin. "Still not big on pain?" She scowled at me, but I ignored her. "Look on the bright side. Whatever happens, there won't be any permanent or fatal injuries." Iseult stuck out her tongue and I chuckled.

"Make yourself comfortable, ladies, no telling how long we'll have to wait."

"What?" Iseult nearly shrieked. "How long do you

think it could take? Hours? Days? I don't want to be stuck here for days."

"Relax. This is just the first watch." I rummaged in my satchel as I added, "If they don't show in a few hours, I'll throw up some precautions and delays to distract them, and we'll hop on down to a local pub to wait them out." I pulled a box out of the satchel. "And in the meantime, I brought chocolates."

Iseult's eyes lit up as I opened the box and passed it around. She popped one in her mouth with an expression of bliss, and even Morgan looked more relaxed as she nibbled on the chocolate.

I selected a hazelnut sweet and sat down on a hunk of the broken dais. I leaned forward and asked, "So where have you been, Iseult, and what have you been up to all these years?" before popping the candy in my mouth and chewing on the confection.

I heard a stifled giggle from Morgan as Iseult frowned. Yet she answered. "This and that. Settled down for a while, as you know, with Martin's grandfather. He died young, and I raised our daughter, Lucy, on my own."

Sadness crossed her face. "I left England when she was in university. Tristan started sniffing around again, the bastard. I went to France after that. I didn't want my daughter exposed to his behaviour or to get mixed up in my mess. I tried to keep in touch, but I don't think she forgave me. I know she blamed magic. She refused to see me for years and wouldn't let me meet Martin. I've kept watch over them, but only from afar. I had to sneak into her funeral five years ago like a stranger." She flopped down on the floor, staring at me, her face a mixture of bitterness and regret.

I swallowed the last bit of my second chocolate with some regret of my own. "I'm sorry. This life of ours is lousy sometimes." I held out the box. She leaned over and snatched another candy. "Your daughter knew about you being a witch?"

Iseult nodded. "I kept her out of the life but she knew. She never told Martin though. I was surprised to find out he became a wizard."

I grunted. "He had help. But if your daughter didn't like magic why leave your spellbook behind when you left?"

"I didn't." She shrugged. "It just disappeared one day,

about two years ago. I didn't even know Martin had it until I found out he was with you."

"It disappeared? What do you mean it disappeared?" Morgan suddenly chimed in on the conversation. "Spellbooks don't just vanish."

"I thought Tristan took it." Iseult lowered her head. "I was back in England at the time, on the run from that loon again. I came back to my hotel one evening and something felt wrong, as if someone had been there. When I searched, my spellbook was gone."

"Interesting." I tapped my finger on the rock as I considered possibilities. "Looks like we should have a talk with your grandson when we get back. We may have to add thief to his resume."

"You think Martin stole it?" Iseult tried to sound shocked but I didn't buy her act. Morgan groaned in the background.

"How else did he get his hands on it?" I asked. "I think you know that, Iseult."

She nodded, hesitant, but accepting. "It just doesn't make sense to me. Lucy refused to accept the magic, so how did he find out?"

"Another question we'll have to ask him." I licked melting chocolate off a finger.

"It seems that quiet, bumbling Martin has some hidden depth." I turned. Morgan leaned against the wall, scuffing the dirt with her boot. "Family always surprises you and disappoints."

"Thinking of Morgawse?" The words tumbled from my mouth without thought and I cursed my slip.

"Never stopped. Not since you rang this morning." She snuffled, letting out a loud exhale. "Only since this morning, and my life is upside down again. I thought I was done with her. I had more than enough lifetimes of making excuses and cleaning up her messes."

She curled her fingers into a fist but didn't say anything. I knew her well enough to let her rage and vent when it came to her sister. Iseult chose to be more vocal.

"If I've learned anything over the years, it's that we cannot control the actions of other people and we can't blame ourselves for the horrible things they do. I used to think Tristan and Mark's behaviour was my fault. I caused it. But

I didn't. I wish I had been more like you. Stood up to them. Fought them better. But I didn't." She let out a small sigh. "The only thing either of us can do is live with our choices, our regrets, and the consequences of their actions."

Morgan didn't reply and an uncomfortable silence settled over the chamber, mixed with the scent of chocolate. I squirmed on my rock, staring at a pebble on the floor. Morgan finally broke the hush.

"Tell me you brought some booze in that satchel of yours."

I gave her a grin. "Well, I did pack a—" I stopped talking as a scrawl of light flashed from the other end of the passageway, inside Arthur's tomb.

"They're here." I swallowed and pulled the last vial out of my bag, instead of the tiny bottles of whisky I had stashed. I nodded at the other women. "Drink your potions."

We unstoppered our bottles and swallowed the contents. Morgan and Iseult moved to their places in the corridor, tucked into concealed niches, and I took up watch in the shadows of the chamber. I kept my eyes on where the passage joined Arthur's Tomb until two cloaked figures, a male and female, moved into view.

I held my breath as the pair strode forward, drawing ever nearer to the place where Iseult and Morgan waited, secreted on opposite sides of the corridor. Suddenly the woman paused, letting the other figure walk ahead. She pushed back her hood, and a flicker of light identified her as Morgawse.

Morgan shifted position and jumped out from hiding. She slammed a ball of magical energy directly into Morgawse, knocking her sister back onto her arse. Iseult leapt forward, threw a follow-up spell at Morgawse, and the three-way fight was on.

I kept my eyes on the male figure. He hesitated, but only for a second. He abandoned Morgawse to her fate and hurried toward the empty chamber where I waited. The sound and sizzle of magic being exchanged rebounded behind him as he moved swiftly along the corridor.

The passage radiated with clashing energy, the acrid scent of singed rock and flashes of light that signalled a fierce fight. I saw snatches of the three tussling and hoped Morgan and Iseult were holding their own. As the man drew closer, I recognized his face in the dim light. Nostradamus had indeed returned.

My heart sank in disappointment. Until now I had secretly hoped I would be proven wrong, that Michel was not behind the abduction of Morgawse. I felt his peculiar power radiating off the stone, far stronger than the last time I knew him. Whoever he was now, he was not the man I remembered.

As he entered the chamber, I stepped into his path, my hand reaching into my satchel. "Hello, Michel."

He halted his progress and stood as still as the rock that surrounded him. He pushed back the hood of his cloak, surprise on his face.

"Nimue. *Bonjour, mon amie.*" The French slipped off his tongue in the honeyed tones I loved, before he surprised me by switching to English, "You are not who I expected, but you were always the unpredictable one."

"A bit unpredictable yourself. A new language and apparently a new lust for power." My finger tightened around a charm inside my bag.

Hurt flashed into his expression. "Is that what you

think this is? Some bourgeois attempt to gain power? You know me better than that, *mamour*, this is far more important than some mere personal gain or trifle of ego."

"I thought I knew you," I replied. "And yet, here you are, seeking the Grail," I added, acid accusation in the words.

With disappointment in his eyes he said, "Where did your belief in me go? Has it faded over the years, so that you believe my motives so base? You are eager to protect the Grail, yet ask me nothing of my reasons in seeking its power? If you knew why, you would stand aside and let me pass."

I ground my teeth. I had almost forgotten his superior airs. I sneered. "What motivation could justify the use of the Grail? It's too powerful for *any* person to control." I moved forward but he held his ground.

Then he said, "I need it to save the world from destruction."

I gaped at him. I had no words. I did not expect *that* answer.

Michel stepped closer. "I had a vision, sweet one. Now I have a mission. I need the Grail. Where did you hide it? Where is the Grail?"

I moved my hand from the satchel, a charm tucked inside, before I answered, "It's gone, where no one can ever find it again. It left here some time ago. You're far too late to find the Grail, Michel."

Anger flared in his eyes, and he shouted, "*Non*! You lie! This is a trick, a ruse to delay me. We have no time for such nonsense. Give me the Grail!" He reached out and grabbed my arm, but I squeezed the charm as his fingers tightened. He yelped, letting go as if his fingers were on fire. Which is probably how they felt. Protection charms burn like the dickens.

I gave him my best glare. "Hands to yourself, Michel." He frowned but had the decency to look contrite. "And I'm not lying. The Grail's gone and there's nothing either of us can do about it. So why don't you stop the bluster and tell me what you think is going on." I softened my tone. "Maybe I can help."

For a moment he hesitated, then, "No, you would not understand, and would not agree to what must be done. I must find another way." Before I could react, he conjured an energy ball and tossed it my way. I clutched the protection charm as it hit me, but still got slammed to the floor.

I scrambled to my feet, cursing my aching muscles, and chased after him as Michel dashed back along the corridor. Just ahead of us, Iseult was slumped against a wall and Morgawse and Morgan were trading magic and punches. I opened my mouth to shout a warning but never got the chance. Michel slammed a bolt of energy at Morgan. She flew across the corridor and tumbled into Arthur's tomb.

Michel shouted something in French and at the far end of the passage a portal appeared, slicing across the air. He raced towards it, faster than I thought possible for him, grabbing Morgawse as he fled. They charged through the exit and vanished.

"Spit and hell! They escaped!" I wanted to hit something. "Damn it! How did he do that? He created a portal with just a spoken spell." A groan from Iseult caught my attention and I moved to her side, helping her to her feet. I glanced over at Morgan as she stumbled back into the passageway, but she seemed more furious than hurt.

I turned back to Iseult. "Are you okay? Anything broken?"

"No." Her voice shook a bit but sounded strong. "Just got the wind knocked out of me by one of Morgawse's energy bolts. She got lucky, that's all."

"It was more than that." Morgan's voice sliced into the conversation coated in anger and bitterness. "She was stronger than before. Much more powerful. Before today, we've always been an even match in our magical abilities. With that boost you gave us and Izzy's help, she should have gone down easily. She didn't. She took out Iseult and I barely held my own. Something's changed."

I frowned, thinking. "It sounds like she had a power boost of her own. *His* doing most likely."

"Maybe she thought she'd need it for the Grail?"

"The Grail doesn't respond to power. You know that, Morgawse knows that, as does Michel, um, I mean, Nostradamus." I blushed over my fumble but continued, "And he acted like he expected opposition, just not me." I glanced up at Morgan. "I don't think it was you or Iseult either. I wonder who else is involved." I rubbed my temples, a headache starting.

"Did he say anything else?" Iseult asked, giving me

a sideways look. "Rant about how he was going to conquer the world?"

"No, but he did mention how he was trying to save the world from destruction."

Chapter Four

Lull

After the disaster of our trap, the three of us sat in a Glastonbury pub surrounded by a mixture of locals and tourists drowning our failure in beer and rather good crispy chips; even Iseult asked for a glass, which was unusual. As we ate, I relayed what I had learned, ending with a whispered, "If he truly thinks he's saving the bloody world this won't end with his failure to acquire the Grail."

Morgan grabbed a chip, chewed it slowly, and then said, "So he's a nutter?"

"I don't think so. He had," I glanced quickly at the other patrons, but no one was paying us any heed, "a vision. And with," I lowered my voice even more, "Nostradamus, visions aren't something to dismiss."

"So, now we have to worry about some unknown magical apocalypse?" Iseult hissed. "In addition to two rogue practitioners? And unknown third parties, which may or may not be on our side or possibly have their own horrid agenda?" She grabbed her glass and took a swig of beer.

I nodded. "Basically."

Morgan snorted. "So just another day, just another crisis to avert. Maybe we should start charging."

The corner of my mouth quirked in a half-smile. "Too much paperwork."

Beside me, Iseult made a noise and nearly spit out a mouthful of beer. She glared at both of us. "How can you be this glib? The bloody damn world might be ending."

I raised an eyebrow at her uncharacteristic cursing and said gently, "Morgan and I have dealt with similar situations before, it's just how we cope. We're taking this seriously." I patted her hand. "Don't fret. We can handle this."

Iseult leaned back and exhaled. Then she drained her glass of beer like a docker. "How do you two keep your sanity? Half a day and I'm already frazzled."

Simultaneously, Morgan and I replied, "Practice," and then we all broke down into giggles. A man at the next table scowled at us and I stuck out my tongue at him. He scowled harder before turning back to his fish and chips.

"It may be time to go." I tilted my head to the next table. "Before we attract more attention."

"Perhaps. I have managed to drink more than I usually do." Iseult giggled while I stared at the array of empty glasses on the table. I didn't remember ordering that many.

"How many beers have you had?" I asked, pushing her order of chips closer. "Eat something."

"Two or three glasses I think." She stabbed her food with a fork and devoured the fried potatoes like a ravenous wolf.

Across the table, Morgan chuckled and finished her lunch in a more dainty manner, while I polished off the last of my chips and beer, and wiped the grease and salt from my fingers with a napkin. Then we left the pub.

Outside, we strolled down Glastonbury's streets, taking in the sights.

Iseult remarked, "It certainly has changed, hasn't it?

Since the old days."

"That it has." I huffed. "Everything's changed since the old days."

"But for the better, surely?" Iseult added with surprise in her tone. I must have let too much discomfort slip out with my words.

"In some ways. But there's too much technology for me. It's all mobiles and computers, tweeting and texting. Disembodied voices talking to you from speakers telling you to do this, do that. Even cars telling you how to drive or doing it for you. Bah!" I kicked at a stray pebble.

"Oh, don't get her started on one of her rants," Morgan's voice complained. "I can't take another one of her 'evils of technology' lectures."

I turned and glared at her. "You mock, but people spend more time these days with their machines than they do with actual people. It's not right."

"And here I thought you didn't like people." Morgan grinned at me and I glowered.

"Stop teasing her." Iseult giggled. "She's just an analog witch in a digital world."

"Bollocks to the pair of you." I huffed and crossed my arms. The other two tumbled into laughter. I gave up and threw my arms in the air in a gesture of surrender. "Fine. Hurrah for technology!"

I lapsed into silence as we walked on, listening to Morgan and Iseult chat about some new fashion or other. Ahead of us, I caught snatches of conversation from tourists discussing the historic importance of Glastonbury as if they were a pair of pompous professors instead of a couple of looky-loos. Though, maybe they were professors. Who was I to judge?

I frowned. Seeing Michel had put me out of sorts. And world-ending prophecies didn't help. I needed to get this whole mess sorted out as quickly as possible and get back to my routine.

"Nimue!" Morgan's sharp tone made me whirl around. She stared at me with impatience. "I've been trying to get your attention. I'm not going back with you to the cottage. I'm heading to London. I'm just going to find an empty lavatory, nip in, and portal out." She patted her pocket. "I brought the prepared spell with me, just in case."

I frowned. "Why aren't you coming back? What are you up to, Morgan?"

"Nothing." She squirmed a bit and my frown deepened. "Just had a few thoughts on how to track down my sister. And what I need is in London." She scuffed her boot across the ground.

I took a step closer. "And if you find her? Are you planning to confront her? Alone? Promise me you won't do something that foolish."

Nothing but silence, as she didn't answer me.

"Promise me, Morgan." I kept my tone low but dropped a healthy dose of disapproval and menace in my words.

She looked me in the eyes and took a breath. As she exhaled, she replied, "I promise."

Part of me wasn't sure if I believed her, but let it go. We said goodbye and she left us. Iseult and I walked on. A few minutes later we found our own secluded place and portalled back home.

I SAT in the garden under the hanging lights, researching with a spellbook and admiring the sunset. Strains of the telly came from the parlour and I knew Martin, Iseult, and Vivienne were well-occupied watching some program. I just hoped they hadn't gotten into the whisky, gin, mead, or the wine. I didn't want to go inside later and deal with those three in a drunken state. Not that I wasn't considering a little tipple myself. After today's disaster, Morgan's desertion, and Vivienne's lack of any visions or other progress on discovering our unknown third parties, I was at a loss. And my books weren't shedding any enlightenment on things either. Several tracking spells had failed to locate Michel or Morgawse, and worry gnawed at the back of my mind.

I closed the book with a loud *thud*, and set it onto the table. I rose, deciding to chuck any responsible behaviour and bring a bottle of wine into the parlour so we could all get drunk together. Anything was better than wallowing alone, listening to the wind rustle Merlin's branches.

I turned to leave, when a wisp of light caught my eye. I stiffened. Something was definitely out there.

"Show yourself!" My voice echoed into the twilight

and a shiver prickled the back of my neck. "Whoever, or whatever you are." The wisp of light shimmered, as if in response, but hovered in place with no other answer.

"All right. That's it! No more games!" Irritated, I moved toward the light. "Either show yourself or I'll spell you out of existence." I started whispering under my breath.

The light exploded suddenly in a shower of sparks, but not of my doing. Another message hung in the air, words written in flickering gold across the burnished sky above my roses.

He's coming. Prepare yourself. Do not trust him.

Then the words faded into grey traces of smoke and ash. All thoughts of getting drunk fled. I turned on my heel and marched off to my storage shed. I had spells to prepare and things to mull over. One piece of the puzzle finally clicked. I recognized the magic in the message and its sender. It was Gwenevere. After all these years she had returned.

Chapter Five

Temptation

I prepared for Michel in the darkening night under the wavering illumination of my hanging lights. I left the others to their laughter and the flickering glow of the telly. I knew he was coming for me.

I set out two glasses and a good bottle of Bordeaux. He always appreciated a fine wine. I also added a few runes and protection charms around the garden to ward against a double-cross, in case his intentions were less than honourable. Then I sat down in my most comfortable chair and waited.

He arrived in a quiet manner, out of a soft shimmer of air and blue luminescence, from between the hedgerows outside the back gate. He strolled through the unlocked entrance, down the garden path and sat in the chair opposite me. I reached over and lifted the bottle of wine.

"Would you care for a glass?"

He nodded. "Indeed I would. Such a pleasant evening and company deserve some enjoyable wine."

I poured two generous glasses; we each took one and sipped the Bordeaux.

"The last time we did this was in a small village in Italy before you moved to Salon. A most singular evening as I recall." I smiled at the memory and he returned the gesture.

"I remember. We met three times in Paris after that, *oui*?"

I nodded. "You were a darling of the King by then."

He shrugged. "That became tiresome after a few years, but what can you do? One must obey the capricious nature of royalty." He swirled his wine. "I was saddened when you left the city."

"Some of my Parisian neighbours were whispering rumours about me practicing witchcraft. It seemed prudent to leave."

Michel chuckled. "So righteous they were. If they

only knew the truth."

I set down my wine. "What is the truth? The man I knew dedicated himself to knowledge and helping people. Even after we said that final goodbye in Salon, after we argued over your decision to go through with the immortality ritual, I never dreamed you would end up like this. Not kidnapping power-hungry witches. Not seeking the Grail for his own ends. What happened to you, Michel? What is this all about, and why have you come here tonight?"

"Always the direct one, were you not?" He sipped some wine. "Very well, you deserve the truth, and now it seems you must have it. You are right about the character of this Morgawse. She is unpredictable, selfish, but I needed her for…" He hesitated but did not elaborate. "Best you not know that yet." He drank more wine as I glared.

"Where is she now?" I asked, not sure I wanted to know the answer.

"She received some sort of summons. Her sister, I believe. I can fetch her back when I need to."

A shiver moved along my spine. *Damn Morgan. She promised. And what did he mean, he could fetch Morgawse back?*

"What happened to you? Your magic, it's far more advanced."

"Ah, yes. Years of study within the netherworlds. Such wonders. You should travel there sometime. Perhaps a vacation." Another sip of wine.

Study in the netherworlds? I should have realized. He had talked of it often enough in Paris. "You found a way to harness wild magic, didn't you? Without complex spells or potions? To tap directly into the raw energy matrix without Ascending?"

Nostradamus nodded. "*Oui.* I created a permanent conduit, similar to the method of channelling but without the requirement of a sacred site. It eliminates the need to ascend and gives me considerably more power."

Is that the difference I sensed? I shifted position slightly and asked, "Why? You never went after power before?"

"Not power, knowledge. I see so much more. I know my purpose now." He leaned forward, his eyes reflecting the light and the fierce magic inside him. "I know my true purpose, my calling. I was born to save the world."

"Well, you still have an ego. That hasn't changed." I

snorted, ignoring the hurt that blossomed in his eyes. Then I rubbed salt in the wound. "I know your religious views have sometimes been at odds with the church, but have you forgone it entirely and jumped right to being God?"

He gasped. "How dare you? That's blasphemous." His tone turned angry, bitter. "I am not God, merely his instrument. And you are one to speak of the Church, having never believed in its teachings."

"I never disbelieved in its teachings, only in its corruption, in its narrow-minded ways. Too often it let the good be buried under the rot, and you know that." Our old argument flared up, and I paused, taking a breath. "Nothing, not religion, not politics, gives people the right to judge, to alter lives with their power. Especially if they possess magic." I stared at him, with, I hoped, a look of stern disapproval.

"I told you, I do not do this to gain some personal status, or rule, or become a god!" He raised his voice, his mannerisms agitated. "This is as I have always done! To save lives! We are in danger. All of us that dwell in the world of magic. If I do not do something we will be destroyed. Our existence is under threat!"

"And this all came to you in a vision?" I scoffed, waving my hand dismissively, trying to keep him angry. I reached over and picked up the bottle of wine and refilled his glass. I wanted his guard down and his tongue loose. He drank more wine and I placed the bottle back on the table. "Some mystic prophecy of doom?"

"This is not some flight of fancy. The very fabric of magic, our world, is at stake. There is a corruption, a dark stain, and it is spreading. I must take control of its heart and purge the sin from it, cut out the disease before it stops the pulse of what sustains us. Before we wither and die." He leaned forward, wine sloshing slightly in his glass. "If I do not stop this, what we have become will cease to be. We will be nothing again. Ordinary and nothing. Finite."

I stared at the red liquid in his glass, the intent and meaning of his words dawning in my brain. "You're talking about the end of all magic." I looked up, straight into his eyes. "The end of immortality." A chill ran across my skin.

No more living forever? Back to being mortal? Oh god, I can't believe it. Could this actually be true? Please let it be true.

He nodded.

I sat back in my chair, shock and a thrill of hope racing through my thoughts. The words slipped out. "Would that really be so terrible?"

The question seemed to surprise him and he looked at me with disappointment. "How can you say that? How can you even fathom the loss of magic to the world?"

"If it means the end of this curse of immortality, of being able to age and die and live as I was naturally intended then it's easy to fathom." I reached over and picked up my glass of wine, draining the alcohol down my throat.

Hell, yes I can imagine that. Shit, that's what I've wanted for centuries.

"I never understood that about you, your reluctance to embrace a continued existence." Nostradamus shook his head. "But would you truly sacrifice all the rest for that one wish? Think of it. No magic. No spells, or portals. No wonder, nor visions. Nothing extraordinary in your life."

I closed my eyes.

No trouble. No problems. No dealing with wayward wizards. Sounds like heaven to me.

"I went to your grave, you know." My sudden change

of subject startled him. "Not long after you supposedly died. Some of your remaining family were there. In mourning for a man still alive." I poured more wine. "They grieved for you. Grieved for the man they thought they lost. That's what this life is: loss and deception. Immortality means living a lie. That's why I hate it."

"So we are at odds. I feared as much."

I frowned. "I'm sure you did. You must have known I would be reluctant to help you. Why come tonight? Why seek me out at all? Not still after the Grail, I hope? That's a lost cause."

"No, but you are the best person to turn to for what I do seek. I need Merlin."

I laughed. I couldn't help it. Then I said, "Look behind you."

Puzzled, he turned. "All I see is a tree."

"That shrubbery used to be Merlin. Your luck is running badly, Michel. Whatever you needed him for, he won't be able to help you."

He turned back and gave me an odd look. "I didn't need him, just something he possessed. With him so conveniently incapacitated, acquiring this item may prove easier."

My skin prickled and not from the night air. "And what possession of Merlin's do you want?"

Nostradamus hesitated, and for a moment I thought he wouldn't tell me, but he said, "His grimoire."

I let out a long breath. "Good luck. That went missing some time after he first…" I fumbled for a word, settling on, "disappeared. The book always had a mind of its own. Who knows where it flew off."

"Then you don't have it?" He pursed his lips.

I chuckled. "So that's what this was about. Feeling me out."

"As were you, with me."

I shrugged. "*C'est la vie.*"

He raised his glass in acknowledgement, and for a moment I felt the years melt away. Then the moment snapped and I added, "I can't help you."

"So be it. Together was never our fate, was it?" He put down his glass and stood. "Will you oppose me?"

I looked at him sadly. "I don't know. I think it

may be better to let magic die, but who am I to speak for everyone?" I shrugged. "I will come after Morgawse though. She is my responsibility."

"You are welcome to her when I am done. Until then... *Bon chance.*" He bowed his head and turned to leave. Then he looked back. "Perhaps I can still change your mind. Go to Stonehenge at twilight. Feel its heart. Then you will know what, and perhaps who, I fight."

I watched him walk off and vanish into the darkness.

The sound of the cottage door opening caught my attention and Iseult stepped out from inside.

"Was that Nostradamus?" Her voice sounded puzzled.

"It was. He came to talk." I stood up, collecting the other wine glass and the bottle. "We had some wine and came to an understanding of sorts." I moved forward towards the house. "But we'd better check on Morgan. Her sister paid her a visit tonight as well."

I HANDED Morgan a bag of ice and a large glass of wine, stepping over bits of broken furniture. She took a gulp of the wine and pressed the ice to her bruised face. She hissed at me, "I can't believe she got away. Again!" Beside her on the sofa, Iseult patted Morgan's shoulder in sympathy.

The three of us were in Morgan's swanky flat, among scattered bits of wood and glass and a few scorched walls; the ruin of a busted coffee table and vase, and the aftermath of the confrontation between Morgawse and Morgan.

"What I can't believe is that you broke your promise and tried to rein in your sister on your own. Sending her a summons. What were you thinking?"

"Apparently, I wasn't thinking." She shifted positions with a groan. "I got my bloody arse kicked for going it alone."

"I'm surprised you're still here and she didn't banish you to some netherworld. Why did she even come, if she didn't mean to rid herself of you permanently?"

"She tried her old pattern, tried to recruit me to her side. Said she was on an important mission, that I should join her and that nutter Nostradamus to heal magic and save the world. I didn't believe a word of it. That's when we started fighting. After my third knockdown, she called it a night and portalled out."

"How did she portal? The old-fashioned way? Or like Nostradamus?" I paused, "And she wasn't lying. At least about saving magic."

"What? What do you mean? And she portalled out the usual manner, with a prepared spell. Her power's still boosted though, but not quite as strong as in Glastonbury."

"Hmmm. Interesting. Could be whatever jolt she received is long lasting but wearing off." I started pacing, winding around the debris. "You weren't the only one with a visitor tonight. Nostradamus came calling and was kind enough to explain himself. He believes there is a corruption in magic and it is basically self-destructing. He's out to play the hero and I guess Morgawse is playing along."

"More like playing him until she can turn the situation to her advantage. That sounds more like her."

I shrugged. "Probably."

"Tell her the rest." Iseult's quiet voice prompted from the sofa.

"Yeah. Well, if we stop Nostradamus, magic more or less goes away. And our immortality." Morgan's head jerked up. "Or we can do nothing and let things play out. He said he'd let us have Morgawse when he was finished."

"And you believe him?" Morgan looked at me like I was crazy. "He could be delusional."

"Maybe. But he's directly harnessed wild magic. Without Ascension. He's channelling far more power than we do. He may have better insight."

"So what now? We do nothing and…" Morgan let her words trail off and gave me a strange accusing look. "Are you thinking of trying to stop him? Of letting magic die?"

"I think she is." Iseult's voice sounded off on the accusation bandwagon.

I glared at the two of them. "Of course, I am!" I snapped. "It could mean the bloody end of immortality!"

"And magic." Iseult said softly. "I can't imagine a world without magic."

"Neither can I," added Morgan, who glared back at me. "We can't oppose this! I won't let you actively try to end magic."

I took a breath. "I haven't made up my mind yet. Nostradamus told me to go to Stonehenge at twilight and feel its heart. That I would understand if I did. That's what

I'm going to do tomorrow evening before I decide anything."

"Then I'm coming with you." Morgan drained the rest of her wine. "And so's she." Morgan nodded at Iseult who frowned and said, "I'll come."

I looked at both of them, feeling guilty and irritated. But I replied, "Fine. A road trip then." Spitefully, I added, "By the way, Gwenevere's back."

I revelled in Morgan's shocked open-mouthed expression and tucked the memory away in my head.

Chapter Six

Stonehenge

"Do we have to sneak around like thieves?" Iseult whined in my ear.

Standing on the plain of Salisbury, hidden by magic and glamoured shadows, and sandwiched between her and Morgan, I nodded. "Unless you'd prefer to explain to the tour guides or the police the reason we're here, yes, we do have to sneak around."

Iseult pouted, but I ignored her. I glanced over at Morgan. She had barely spoken to me since I'd mentioned Gwenevere. I turned my attention back to the tour group currently soaking in the wonders of Stonehenge. Just my luck to pick the exact day and time of one of the sunset tours. The bloody tourists were mingling among the stone circle instead of remaining at a safe distance.

Shit. If one of them notices something… but no use whinging, it can't be helped.

"Come on. We'll just have to do this and hope we don't get caught."

We had entered the area along the trail from Woodhenge, so I marched forward towards the standing stones, Iseult and Morgan following. Spells kept us invisible from eyes and ears, but we'd still have to be careful. If we knocked about too much, people might notice things like bent grass or disturbed foliage. Not to mention when I started the real show of connecting with the sacred site; any misstep and unpredictable results might bleed out into our world.

So bloody much could go wrong. Damn tourists.

I counted the heads gawking at the monoliths and asking questions of the bored-looking guides. A small group, manageable enough if things went sideways. I motioned for the other two to slow down, letting the tour group move until the larger stones blocked them from our view.

"They seem to be headed to the other side of the ruins. Hopefully they'll stay there during the spell." I waited, then sprinted across the plain and jumped a fence. I glanced back to make sure the other two were keeping up, then stopped at the back side of the half circle. Morgan and Iseult moved behind me, about a foot away.

"Keep watch," I ordered. "I'm about to begin." I glanced over at the tour group. They were staying put, out of a direct line of sight.

Good. Hopefully they'll stay out of our way.

Morgan and Iseult took flanking positions, their eyes fixed on the tourists. I raised my head, staring at the coloured sky, all cerise and fading blue. I inhaled a breath, exhaled, and placed my hand onto one of the stones. The energy pulsed under my fingers, its wild magic coursing through the rock and into the earth.

I looked down at the grass, at the soil and whispered, "*Danywch eih caloch yn mi.*"

My fingers twitched and the stone warmed under my touch. Beneath my feet, the soil trembled. Sparks snapped around my hand and a frisson of energy flowed into my body, connecting me to Stonehenge and the earth. My head jerked back and the image of the sky cracked open, bridging the divide between worlds. Then I was lost to the heart of the magic.

My essence, my thoughts, and my magic submerged into the energy as if it were water. I idly wondered if this was how Vivienne felt in her lake. I drifted in a sea of colour and stars, of earth and rock, along the sound of trees and wind, past forever souls and mortal endings. I drowned in an eternal web of everything and nothing, lost in the infinite ocean of wild magic.

I floated for who knows how long, bobbing in a sea of patterns laced with strands of power, an ever-expanding filigree that bound all the realms and worlds. Time revolved around me, memories I knew and places I had never been. A whirlwind of kings and paupers, of isolated moments, their meaning known to only a few, and events that changed the course of history. I saw, sensed, experienced eons and seconds simultaneously and it felt glorious. In that moment I understood why Michel had sought a more permanent connection with this elemental force.

I reached out, flowing my essence through the threads that surrounded me, merging myself deeper and deeper into the primal energy. Instinctively I searched, trying to find answers as more and more of my conscious mind merged with the visceral power pulsing through my being. Part of me wanted to let go, unite permanently with the energy, separate from flesh and bone and free myself from any constraints of physical existence. To release myself into a joyous life of drifting amid light and time and peace.

Then I felt it: a buzz, a snap of sparking discord and blackened energy. I traced the anomaly to a cold dark thread; a limp strand of the matrix that smelled of blood. I followed the trail like a fox hound, weaving in and out of centuries, realms, and the universal core of magic to finally alight in a scene of a small woodland somewhere between mortality, the Faerie worlds, and the realm of the elementals. A netherworld, but one I had never seen before, one that sang of sadness, echoed in a broken mourning of eternal melancholy. The bleak emotions dripped off the trees and swirled through the leaves like a sour wind.

In the center of the woods, on a tiny patch of scorched

earth, sat a nymph. The dark thread stemmed from her and this patch of charred ground, and her wave of misery hit me like a runaway lorry. Yet I saw no reason why this darkness had infected the energy matrix until I watched her raise the knife and mouth a spell. I could not hear her words but I knew what she intended.

Blood magic.

The blade sliced across her throat and she died, her blood seeping into the soil along with the desolation that pushed her to this atrocity. Even in a disembodied state, I choked on the contaminating mesh of festering, fetid pain violently impelled into the substance of magic. I gagged as another wave of nausea hit me.

Shit! She's also channelling. Nostradamus was right. That spell will pollute magic and corrupt anything it touches.

I stared at the corpse as it withered across the span of time until the spell circled back and it began again; an eternal cycle of death. An endless loop of despair wrapped in a deliberate act of defiance and a final touch of anarchy. I wondered what had driven the creature to such a horrid self-destruction.

What agony drove you to such lengths? To weave a spell from the constant rebirth of your own death?

I clenched my jaw, fighting back tears, and turned away from the scene.

As I backed away from the tableau of dark futility and waste, I paused, a strange echo vibrating along the dark thread. Without thinking, I touched the reverberation and a shock wave hit me. Hate, fury, and need—stark and visceral—slammed into me with the force of a thunderstorm. I spun along the energy patterns, out-of control and buffeted by an overwhelming frenzy. A monstrous presence loomed inside the fabric of magic, screaming its rage at me. I lashed out, stabbing at the surrounding power with a magical spell burst, desperate to escape. The backlash of intersecting magicks shoved me along another stream of energy and I tumbled away from the threat. Right into another lurking essence.

Underneath the reverberation of the raw emotion, but past its looming primal presence, a voice softly chuckled. At first I thought it might be what I had encountered, but it resonated with a different harmony. Not raw or elemental, but like the shadow of someone human.

"Hello, Nimue." A male voice, deep and raspy.

I shivered. "Who are you?"

"A friend." Another chuckle echoed.

"My friends don't hide in the shadows." Dark energy shimmered in the distance and I shifted position.

"Don't they? But then, they also think immortality and magic are a gift. You and I know better. That's why I'm changing the game."

My breath caught and I blurted, "You're behind all this!"

"Clever girl. You always had a quick mind. And sense enough to know what's best for you. Stop that fool of a Frenchman and let events unfold. Let my plans play out. Then I'll give you what you want. Mortality. A normal life."

That caught my attention. Yet… "It sounds good. Too good," I sneered. "Like a dodgy git trying to sell a used car. What's the catch?"

"Always the suspicious one," he replied. "No catch."

"Bollocks! There's something in it for you." I shifted a bit closer.

"Does it matter? You'll get what you want." The voice

got cranky. "I need an answer."

Annoyance rose in me. "What's your fucking hurry? Got somewhere else to be?"

"Can't you just do what you're asked for once?" His shout shook the surrounding threads. "Stay out of this!"

That provoked me. "I'll do whatever I fucking want, you—"

"Too late." He cut me off and the dark shadow of energy vanished.

"Running away are—" Pain shot through my back and a burst of power slammed me face down into the interwoven threads surrounding me.

A shadowy arm grabbed me around the throat and magic stabbed through my essence. I screamed as his voice boomed, "Bitch! I wanted you as an ally, but I can give you the death you long for! I'll scatter your being across thousands of threads until it becomes impossible for you to exist anymore!"

I convulsed and shrieked as he tried to rip me apart. Instinctively, I shot bolts of energy into the matrix web, twisting and turning to free myself from his grip. I got lucky, as a ricochet struck him and then I shoved the bastard off me.

I scrambled up and finally saw my attacker.

What the fuck? He had no features, his entire astral form a purple-black silhouette.

Rolling with the shock, I lobbed two hits of energy to his dark core sending him reeling to his knees. I closed in to finish him off. But I never got the chance as a new force yanked me away.

I watched the bastard shadow man laugh as I plunged through the matrix energy.

I bounced along the threads of power, coming to a stop somewhere along the boundaries of Stonehenge. Then, in front of me, the strands glowed and reformed into words.

Not yet. It is not time for you to confront him.

As I stared, the figure of Gwenevere appeared, a wavering dreamlike vision. She held out her hand. Her voice spoke to me.

You know enough. Now go back.

She moved forward and I felt a push. I fell back, down, down into my flesh, her parting words echoing in my ears.

Nostradamus doesn't understand. He cannot control

what is happening. Stop him.

Then I descended into darkness.

I opened my eyes and saw the anxious faces of Morgan and Iseult peering down at me. I lay on the ground, a metallic taste in my mouth. As I tried to form thought, a voice echoed in my head.

Destiny begins.

Morgan whispered, "Can you stand? I think we'd best get out of here quickly. I don't think anyone spotted us, but the glamour spell wavered near the end with feedback energy. A few of those tourists looked our way. We shouldn't push our luck."

I scrambled unsteadily to my feet and the other women helped me regain my balance. Then we hightailed back the way we had come and portalled home.

"BLOOD MAGIC!" Morgan threw up her hands, shouting for the umpteenth time. She paced the parlour of my cottage, alternating rants with bouts of brooding. Iseult sat curled up on my sofa, her face a mask of fear, while Vivienne stared into a half-empty cup of tea and whimpered. Martin sat in an armchair and looked confused. I swayed back and forth in my rocking chair.

"Yes. Mixed with ascendant channelling, I think. The spell's recent too. Not more than a few months by the feel of it." I closed my eyes for a moment, remembering. "It sounds mad, I know, but some practitioner deliberately engineered the sacrifice of a nymph to contaminate the fabric of magic. What's even more disturbing is that the nymph was a willing participant. She cycled her misery and death for infinity." I shivered. "That's obscene."

"Ascendant blood magic," Vivienne murmured from the sofa. "Fueled by a self-sacrificial act, sustained by pain. A powerful spell. I know..." She looked at me as she stopped talking. I made a mental note to question her later regarding what she wasn't telling us.

Morgan's voice broke into the awkward pause. "How long do you think before everything goes to shit?"

"It's not progressing with any speed, though I suspect the more it corrupts the faster it will spread. I'd say a few months, maybe."

Morgan stopped pacing and tapped her foot. "Enough time to find a solution then." She resumed her pacing. "Any idea who this other wizard, influence, whatever, is?"

"No. Other than he was a mean wanker." I rubbed my throat. "Gwenevere pulled me out before I could torture him for answers."

"Gwenevere!" Morgan spat the name. "Why did she have to be involved? I thought she was locked up in a convent?"

"I'm betting she's been far more active than we thought these last few centuries. I think she's up to her earlobes in this mess." I crossed my arms as Morgan glowered. "Relax. She's staying in the shadows for now. Besides, isn't Lancelot off on that natural health retreat with Gawain? No need to be jealous quite yet."

"Jealous! Of that slag? You can't be…" She glared as she spotted my smirk. "I'm not jealous. Lance is over her."

"Gwenevere left him behind long ago." Vivienne's singsong voice cut through our banter and I turned to see her in a trance-like state. "She's found a new home. In the shadows and beyond. Warden. Protector. But of what? Of what?" She paused and her expression transformed with a dreamlike quality. Then she continued, "Webs of power, webs of lies. Guardians and kings, spinning round the wheel. Soon we will all feel it. Soon it will surface. First the netherworlds. Then the mystic sites. Then it will infect us all." With the last word, she slumped against the sofa cushions, barely keeping her tea from spilling in her lap. She moved her head from side-to-side, her eyes turning white and whispered, "Why didn't I sense it? Why didn't I know? They protected. She protected. They shielded the world. The Wardens. The Wardens have always been there."

"Viv?" I spoke softly, quietly as if to a frightened child. "Are you all right?"

She looked up at me. "She is a warden. Watching. Waiting. Gwenevere is in the middle of everything." Then she lapsed into silence and refused to say another word.

I sighed. "Let's call it a night." I gave Morgan, Iseult, and Martin a look. Morgan huffed but left the parlour. Iseult followed her without a word to me. Martin trailed his grandmother but turned back at the door, asking, "You're going to save magic, aren't you?"

I looked at his sad eyes with more than a twinge of guilt. I managed a pathetic nod and he left, looking less than reassured.

"I don't know. The Wardens have secrets I don't know." From the sofa, Vivienne's confused voice dared me to question her.

I flexed my fingers. I needed to tread carefully. "I don't care about your wardens. Not now. I want to know about the blood magic spell." I turned and stared straight at Viv. "What do you know about that?"

Vivienne drained the last of her tea before answering, placing her cup down on a side table. "Only what he told me. About a spell he created. Called it the Blood Sacrifice. But he wanted to use it to control the wild magic and the matrix, not corrupt it. That's something new." Vivienne wrung her hands and stared at the ground. "He never used it. Not once. He said it was too dangerous."

I inhaled sharply, and asked, "Who created the spell?"

She looked at me as if she wouldn't answer, but then replied, "Merlin."

Suddenly it made sense. "That's why Michel wants his

grimoire now that the Grail's out of his reach. He thinks the spell's inside. He probably wants to use it to break this version of the Blood Sacrifice or reverse it." I frowned. "I wonder how Michel knew?" I looked at Vivienne. "Did you or Merlin tell anyone else?"

"I think Arthur knew something, maybe he told Gwenevere."

"That could explain some things, but not how Michel got involved." I frowned. "Maybe he had a vision. A question for another day I guess." I rose. "Come on Viv, let's get some rest. It's going to be a long day tomorrow."

Chapter Seven

Spellbooks

I awoke to the smell of frying bacon. With a rumbling stomach and a hope that Morgan wasn't the one cooking I got out of bed and put on a robe. I walked down the stairs and into the kitchen to see Martin making breakfast. A lot of breakfast. Bacon, sausage and eggs, and pancakes. A big plate of toast, jam, and a pot of tea.

"Oh, you're up. The others are still asleep I think." Martin gave me a half smile. "I woke up early so I decided to cook."

I shrugged and grabbed a piece of toast, slathering on some jam. I took a bite, with a touch of surprise. "Is that Millie's jam recipe?" I asked.

Martin nodded. "She sent it in her last letter."

I took another bite of bliss. I missed Millie. Her departure was why I had shut down the holiday let business. "I still can't believe she retired and moved to Cornwall with her daughter and grandkids."

"Yeah. But she seems happy. At least her letters seem that way."

"I'm glad." I reached for another piece of buttered toast as footsteps sounded behind me. Morgan's voice asked, "Is that bacon?"

"And sausage." Martin dished up the meat onto a platter and set it on the island. Morgan grabbed some toast and slapped some bacon between the slices to make a sandwich. I snitched a sausage for my second piece of toast and poured myself a cup of tea.

More footsteps sounded, and soon Vivienne and then Iseult pulled chairs up to the kitchen table. They filled their breakfast plates with stacks of pancakes and jam, sausages and toast. I added some eggs to my plate as we all settled down to eat. Martin sat at the island counter with me, picking at his eggs and bacon.

"What's going to happen now?" We all looked at Martin over mouthfuls of food. He stabbed a sausage but continued. "What are we going to do? This is all so much. Everything depends on what we do. Or don't do." He pushed his sausage against his eggs breaking the yolks. I watched the yellow goop drip across the plate. "I mean, isn't Nostradamus trying to help? If we stop him, won't bad things happen?" Martin glanced at all of us. His eyes reminded me of a hurt puppy. Then he asked, "Are we going to let magic die?"

I knew without looking that the others were staring at me, expecting an answer. I gave them the best one I could. "This blood sacrifice spell changes things to be certain. Blood magic can have erratic consequences, even on its own and not combined. I don't think sitting back and letting things play out is an option anymore." I heard an intake of breath from someone. "Plus, there's that shadowy plonker of a wizard behind all this. I want to see him fry." I crunched down on my toast and violently chewed a bite. "Not sure if we can let Nostradamus have free rein, though. Gwenevere," I paused as Morgan grunted, "said he couldn't fix the problem."

"So what do we do?" Iseult threw her question into the

discussion. I was beginning to see the resemblance between her and Martin.

"I think we need to search for Merlin's grimoire." I dropped that bombshell and took a bite of my sausage.

While Iseult and Morgan stared at me, and Vivienne busied herself stuffing pancakes into her mouth, Martin asked, "Why don't you just ask Granny where it is?"

It was my turn to stare, while egg yolk dripped from my toast sandwich onto the plate. I turned my head slowly, glaring at Iseult. "What is he talking about?"

She seemed confused. "I have no idea. Honestly. Why would I know anything about Merlin's grimoire?"

I turned back to Martin, but he glared at his grandmother. "It's in your spellbook. I mean, it mentioned the words, 'Merlin's Grimoire', at least. But that's the only bit that was in English. I didn't understand the rest of the page. It was written in some weird foreign language or something. Even the online translators couldn't recognize it." He glanced at all of us. "Elaine couldn't decipher it, either. She was mad about that."

"Iseult!" I dropped my soggy toast and the fork

clattered against my plate. My shout and the noise made everyone jump. "How the bloody hell did a reference to Merlin's grimoire and some ancient jargon get into your spellbook? What the hell have you been up to?"

"I don't know how it got there!" Iseult fluttered her hands, clearly distressed. "I never saw a page like that when I had it. I certainly never added that page. Someone else…" She stopped talking as our eyes met. I'm fairly certain the same thought raced through both our minds.

I looked at Martin. "How exactly did you get Iseult's spellbook?"

"In the mail. With a note from Granny." Another expression of confusion crossed his face. I felt sorry for him. He looked over at Iseult. "Didn't you send me the book?"

"No," Iseult whispered. "The last time I saw that book was in a hotel room. Someone stole it from me."

"Then who sent it?" Martin gulped, fear blossoming on his face. He grabbed his teacup, slurping a big swallow of the liquid down his throat. After a little choking, a napkin wipe and a few panicked breaths later he calmed down.

I asked, "Do you still have the note?"

Martin nodded. "In my things."

"Can you go fetch it, please?"

"Okay." He slipped out of his chair and trotted upstairs.

As soon as he was out of earshot, Iseult whimpered to me, "Have you seen this page he mentioned?"

I shook my head. "But I haven't studied the book, just glanced through it. He's protective of it, and most of what we've worked on isn't as advanced as what is in your spellbook." I flicked a crumb on my plate. "It's not like I can use the book, anyway. You did a good job of protecting it with the bloodline enchantment."

"What's going on?" Iseult's voice sounded small and scared. "Who stole my book and sent it to Martin? What are we involved in?"

A grunt came from Morgan and she added, "A better question is, what do they know about Merlin and his grimoire? And why hide the knowledge in your spellbook? More secrecy and nonsense."

"Wardens maybe." Vivienne glanced up from her dwindling stack of pancakes. "Their motives can be odd." She stuffed a forkful of food in her mouth and chewed.

"I doubt it." I half-glared at Vivienne, still in the dark about these 'wardens' but knowing she wouldn't give up any information. "Assuming you're talking about Gwenevere or anyone she's working with, why would they need us if they knew about the grimoire? Wouldn't they simply use Merlin's book and fix the problem?"

Vivienne tilted her head as if considering my words. Or listening to something else beyond. All she said was, "Maybe, maybe not."

I sighed, but continued. "I think it is more likely it's yet another player in our game."

A clomping down the stairs interrupted us and a few minutes later Martin entered the kitchen carrying Iseult's spellbook and a folded piece of paper.

He plunked the book on the counter and handed the letter to me. I opened it and gave it a quick once over before reading it out loud.

Dearest Martin,

I know we have never met, but you are and always will be my family. As such, I wanted you to have my legacy. This book is a family heirloom and it is time it was passed on to you. I know you will do your family proud and use the secrets within these pages wisely.

Your loving grandmother, Iseult.

I looked over at Martin. I'd seen grieving mothers look happier.

"I thought she wrote it. I thought she wanted me to have it. I thought she believed in me."

"Oh, I do!" Iseult exclaimed. She jumped up and rushed to Martin's side. She hugged him, to his delight and my embarrassment. "I do believe in you."

"Okay fine." I waved the fake note in irritation. "Enough with the affirmations."

Iseult grinned and let go of her grandson. I handed her the note, while Martin started flipping through the pages of the spellbook. "It looks like your handwriting to me. What do you think of it?"

She glanced at it with a frown. "You're right. It does look like I wrote it. But I didn't."

I took the note back and studied it for a minute. "It doesn't feel like magic. Maybe just a good old-fashioned forgery. But why, I wonder. Martin wouldn't have known your handwriting from a stranger's."

"I found it!" Martin's triumphant shout distracted me from my musings, and I set the note down. Iseult and I leaned over for a look at the mysterious page and I felt Morgan and Vivienne press in behind us straining for a peek.

"See there," Martin poked his finger about halfway down the page. "Merlin's Grimoire."

And sure, enough, the two words stood out among the spidery handwriting surrounding it. I examined the script more closely, memories flitting around in my brain. Then it clicked.

"It's the bloody language of the Fisher King! The page is written in the language of the Fisher King." I pushed past them all, hurrying out of the room to a chorus of "the what?" I raced upstairs to my bedroom closet, robe and slippers flapping, and rummaged around until I found an old tattered box. I withdrew a battered notebook and raced back downstairs. Everyone waited, in a state of confusion. I waved the notebook.

"It's code. Some daft thing Perceval invented back in the 1620s, before his first bout of insanity."

"Yeah," Morgan said, "I remember he lived with the Fisher King back then."

"Yes. They were both convinced someone was spying on them and Perceval created a new language to disguise their correspondence."

"So how did you discover it?" Iseult asked.

I shrugged. "Who do you think was spying on them?"

"So do you think Perceval," Iseult shot me a worried look, "or the Fisher King did this?"

"Neither one. Perceval doesn't have the brains, and the Fisher King is in America running one of those daft cults in the woods somewhere. Perceval's not one to keep his mouth shut when he's not in his right senses. It probably wouldn't have been hard for someone to get him to spill."

I flipped open the notebook to review it quickly and then studied the spellbook page, referring to the notes as I did so. After a few minutes, I looked up.

"I may need time to figure all this out. There's been

some tweaking here and there. I did make out a few things, though." I pointed to the short paragraph that alluded to Merlin and his book. "This section says something like 'Spirited away in the night, I retrieved the book from the prison. It is now beyond everyone's greedy hands.' I guess that's how the grimoire vanished after Merlin was trapped in the cave."

Vivienne snorted behind me but I didn't comment, only continuing, "I think the next part says, 'The temptation to keep the book was great, but the Lady convinced me otherwise.'" I frowned, glancing over at Vivienne but she shook her head and mouthed, 'not me'. "'So I have hidden Merlin's grimoire, and…'"

As I said those words, the page suddenly glowed, every letter transforming, shifting, lifting off the page to reform. When the light faded the entire page was written in English.

Martin shrieked, "Holy shit!"

I smiled. "Indeed, Martin, indeed."

"So read it already!" Morgan's exasperated shout made me chuckle, but I put Martin's note in the page and shut the book.

"After breakfast, in the garden. With some tea and wine, and a good shower. I think we will need that."

Chapter Eight

Netherworlds

Late morning we were all gathered in the garden with a pot of tea spiked with whisky, and a plate of scones and jam. Iseult's spellbook was open on my lap.

"This first paragraph or so is just going on about Merlin being a wanker. At least whoever wrote this was a good judge of character." Morgan chuckled and leaves rustled in the background. "Oh, wait. This bit is interesting. Could be about your mysterious wardens, Viv." I looked at her, hoping she would explain her cryptic remarks.

Vivienne shrugged, and said, "Read it."

"'They styled themselves defenders of magic, these nine women, and came to me for help. I knew many of them well, and others only by name. They called themselves the Daughters of Avalon.'" I jerked my head up and shot an accusing glare at Morgan. "The Daughters of Avalon? Those are your old cronies. Care to spill, Morgan?"

She stared back with a look I could only call flabbergasted. "I wasn't part of this. Whoever those nine ladies were, I wasn't there."

I frowned. "But there were only nine, correct, including you?"

Morgan nodded. "So I thought. I was wrong, apparently. Or maybe this happened after I left."

"You didn't leave the Daughters until after the Normans invaded. Gwenevere replaced you though..." I tapped the edge of the book with a finger. "No. That doesn't fit. The grimoire vanished centuries earlier."

"Can someone clue me in?" Martin piped up. "Who are the Daughters of Avalon?"

I tilted my head at him. "A secret Camelot coven, nine witches based out of Glastonbury, back in the day. Morgan, Ygraine, Ragnell, Enid, Luned, Gwenddydd, Dindrane, Elen, and Ana. And apparently at least one other woman we are not aware of."

"Maybe Gwenevere?" Martin replied. "She could have been involved with the group earlier than you thought."

My finger stopped tapping. "Maybe. It would be like her to gradually worm her way in."

"We can speculate later; keep reading." Iseult's irritated voice interrupted and I turned back to the book.

"Not much more on them, just that they came back a couple of times, testing how far they could trust this person whoever he is, and then the day they revealed what they wanted him to—oh this is interesting. They're the ones behind the theft of the grimoire. They asked him to steal it for the Daughters of Avalon."

"Why those dirty rotten louses!" Morgan jumped up and started pacing. "That's why they cut me out. They didn't want me having access to the book."

"Can you blame them?" She whirled and gave me the stink-eye. I stuck out my tongue and snapped, "Come on, Morgan, you get a bit possessive around powerful spellbooks, especially back then. Sit down and stop fussing."

She plonked her arse back in her chair and I went back

to scanning the book. Martin's voice brought my attention back to the group.

"But he didn't do it, though, he didn't hand it over to them. That first paragraph you read, the magic one, said so."

"You're right. Let's find out why." I scoured the page. "Hmmm, he did steal it, though. I'll skip over the bits about the theft, although it was clever. I wonder why he didn't turn it over to the Daughters? Oh… listen to this." I cleared my throat, and read:

"I opened the grimoire. I couldn't help myself. All those spells, all that power. But it was so much more, so much beyond what I thought. I wanted to keep it, so I fled. I took the book and thought to hide it far away from the Daughters, even become what Merlin failed to be. Then I had the dream. She showed me what I had to do, that the grimoire was not for me. Yet, it was not for the Daughters either, though they schemed to have it. I hid the book as she asked. Past the now and waiting for the seeker."

Inwardly I groaned. Another bloody riddle. I hated riddles. I kept reading.

"I speak to you with these words, seeker, find me and

I will give you the key to the garden of Caer Wydyr."

I looked up at everyone. "Shit."

"What?" Martin's head bobbed, glancing at us, anxiety in his voice.

"Caer Wydyr is in the Otherworld, netherworld of the gods, in the realm of Annwn. One of the hidden places of the Tylwyth Teg." I smacked the arm of my chair. "How the hell do we go there? There's only one way I know to find an entrance, and it's dangerous." I shivered at the thought of locating the Cwn Annwn and persuading one of those hounds to help. "If this nut who wrote this has some special key, how the bloody hell do we find him?"

"Keep reading, maybe there are more clues." Iseult tried to sound reassuring, but it sounded more desperate.

I scanned the book, skipping over the incessant parts that rambled on praising the 'Lady' until… "Hold on, this bit gets good. 'The Lady gives me guidance to change my ways and make amends to the one I have wronged but I have often ignored her. Today I will cease this behavior. With my actions, and the words on this page, I vow to mend the rift with Iseult.'" She gasped and I read the rest, "'Bring Iseult to me, Nimue the seeker, bring her to her former husband and I will hand you the key.'" A chill ran down my spine.

Iseult jumped to her feet as I finished, screaming. "You're not taking me to see that bloody fucking Mark! Not if the whole damn world ends!" She stormed out of the room and Martin scurried after her.

I shut the book with a sigh. "I didn't expect that."

"Iseult's reaction or that Mark is behind the disappearance of Merlin's grimoire?" Morgan asked, sarcasm slicing around the edges of her words. "Because I'm surprised Izzy took the news *that* well."

"The grimoire. And who's pulling his strings? The Mark I knew would have used Merlin's spellbook in a heartbeat. Not hidden it and set up some elaborate game of hide-and-seek."

"Yeah," Morgan agreed, "he was always a right bastard, and not one for taking orders from women. That must have been one hell of a dream."

"You're missing the crucial point." Vivienne soft voice interjected. "How did Mark know? About Nimue? He called her 'the seeker' and he knew she would be looking for the grimoire at some point. And that Martin would become your apprentice. Otherwise, why send him Iseult's spell book? You're the one who transformed the page. Not Martin. He was just a means to an end for Mark's objective. The true message, the one about the grimoire, was meant for you." She smirked at me before continuing, "This 'Lady', whoever she may be, is most definitely a seer."

I gaped at Vivienne. Sometimes I forgot how clever she truly was and how much she saw beyond the realms. I asked, "Any idea who?"

She shook her head. "It could be any one of us. Several seers have gone by some variant of 'The Lady', over the years, including me."

"Great. A cadre of candidates, then." I slumped forward. "All these people pulling strings. I'm getting a bit sick of it." I glanced at the door to the cottage. "I suppose we'd better go after Iseult and calm her down. Key or no key, I'm not making her go anywhere she doesn't want to go." I rose and set the spellbook down in the chair. Vivienne and Morgan got to their feet as well.

As we left the garden, Morgan asked, "Do you even

know where Mark is these days?"

I nodded. "He's back in Tintagel. Set up a cozy pocket netherworld under the site, with access out in the middle of the ruins."

"YOU DON'T have to go near Mark." I tried to sound reassuring and make myself heard over her sobbing and screeching. Martin patted her hand and behind me Vivienne and Morgan scuffled their feet.

"I won't see him! I won't!" She didn't seem to hear me or maybe she didn't believe me. "Why did he come back? I thought I was finally rid of that man. Years! It has been years since he tried to worm his way back into life and now this? Fucking trying to blackmail me into going to see him." She suddenly turned on me and glared. "And if you try to force me, or make me feel guilty, I'll—I'll turn you into a frog!" She crossed arms with a look on her face that dared me to try.

I repressed a grin. It would be a cold day in hell before Iseult could turn me into anything. I tried again to get her to hear me. "I'm not making you do anything—" A shriek interrupted me. For a moment I thought Iseult had started up again. Then I realized the scream came from Vivienne and I whirled around.

Her body stiffened before my eyes, her posture rigid and her head jerked back. She screamed again, a loud, infernal shriek of terror. She collapsed to her knees shouting the words, "*Abyssus abyssum invocat,*" and the room around us shook like a terrier with a rat. Books tumbled off the shelf and I barely caught the lamp before it crashed to the floor.

As the rumbling stopped, Vivienne screamed again and shouted, "No, no! You don't know what you're doing! No!"

Morgan and I rushed to her side and she grabbed my arm, digging her fingers into my flesh. "He's going to destroy it." She gasped, her eyes bright blue and wild-looking. "A netherworld. We have to stop him." She whirled on Martin. "Water. I need water now!" He scurried off like his arse was on fire.

I tried to calm her down. "It's all right Vivienne, we'll figure it out whatever is going on." Her fingers tightened on my arm. I winced.

"No, no. We have to go now."

Martin rushed back into the room carrying a glass of water. Vivienne grabbed it, spilled the water onto the floor and threw away the glass. She reached out and grabbed Morgan. Before I could stop her, she chanted, "*Aragor, wyn, gorchmyn.*"

The puddle of water swirled and a portal opened up around us; straight access to a netherworld. I cursed, trying to pull back, but it was too late.

And then we were gone.

We tumbled down into a dark damp space showering sparks all around us. I looked up, saw only Morgan and Vivienne, and yelled, "What the bloody deuced hell?"

Morgan scrambled to her feet and grabbed Vivienne. "What the hell were you thinking? Where did you bring us? What the hell is going on?"

"He's destroying it. He's destroying it. We have to stop him." Vivienne babbled like a lunatic, pointing to the long dark passage that lay ahead of us. The ground, if you could call it ground, rumbled under our feet and flares of light suddenly lit the space around us.

"Come on," I shouted. "Whatever is going on is up

this way." I dashed forward, hoping the others would follow, relieved when footsteps sounded behind me. Then a familiar figure raced down another corridor.

Shit! It's Morgawse.

I hesitated, but the sound of another voice pulled my attention away and I raced towards it. The three of us emerged in a grotto and came face-to-face with Nostradamus.

He was in the midst of a spell. One I recognized.

"Fucking shit!" I rushed forward, only to realize we were too late. "Get down!" I shouted to Morgan and Vivienne, who were still by the entrance. And then the world around us exploded in flashing bursts of light and sound.

Morgan and Vivienne tumbled back into the passageway and I was thrown against the back wall. Dazed, I watched helplessly as Nostradamus drained the energy of the netherworld and then channelled the power into his body.

"Stop!" I shouted. "You don't know what you're doing. You could destroy all the realms. The netherworld connections are too fragile. Draining one could make the others collapse."

He didn't listen and within minutes, the world

convulsed, its substance disintegrating around us. Cracks snapped across the realm space above our heads and magic energy burst like fireworks from the grotto walls, the ground, and every inch of the netherworld matrix.

Then black sparks snapped across the cracks as the dark magic corruption leaked through.

"Shit, it's destabilizing!" I scrambled to my feet, yelling at Michel, "You're channelling the corrupted energy as well as the normal matrix!" My warning came too late. Nostradamus screamed in agony and an onyx fire sheathed his body.

I shouted at Morgan and Vivienne. "You two get out! I'll handle this."

"No!" Morgan snapped back. "You can't do this alone!"

"Morgawse is here." I knew that would work. "She took the left corridor we passed. Find her and get out!"

Morgan hesitated, and then grabbed Vivienne and fled. I looked over at Nostradamus, his face contorted, as the world exploded around us in amber and obsidian. Then I closed my eyes.

I scrambled to breathe and reached out to the wild,

pulsing magic core of the storm. I channelled the immense power and shouted, "By the earth and through the stone. Rise from fire and knit the bone. *Gwydar thyawyn! Tyllwych dyw! Tyllwych dwr!* Cleanse the taint and break the threads!"

For a moment nothing happened. Then the power snapped through me like lightning and I felt my body spasm. I rode on the wave of the connected netherworlds, my thoughts and magic spinning into the vortex. Around me, the tethers that bridged the worlds frayed and snapped, sparking loose energy within the surrounding spaces. And at the edges crackled black flares of tainted magic.

Shit!

Then the power of my own spell surged and I reached out, yanking at the broken threads, drawing them away from the contaminated energy, knitting them back together, and excising the corrupted connections. I wove them back together strand by strand, bypassing the drained netherworld and avoiding the dark magic, and cleaved Nostradamus' connection to the magic. I knew it wouldn't hold back the incursion of tainted magic forever, but it would keep reality from collapsing.

I shrieked in perverse triumph as the magic of the netherworlds realigned and settled back into normality. The surrounding landscape faded in illumination, turning into a sooty husk of what it once was. I severed my connection to the magic and let it flow back into the netherworld realm. Nostradamus fell to his knees as I stood there shaking. Somehow I found my voice.

"What were you thinking? Destroying a netherworld!" I spat. "And almost getting yourself trapped in the tainted spell. You used to be more careful than that!"

Nostradamus pulled himself to his feet, leaning against a wall. Its surface crumbled slightly under his hand. "I was cutting out the disease! Purging a part of the corruption before it could spread further!"

"And how well did that work?" I sneered. "You nearly destabilized this section of the realms."

Nostradamus ground his teeth. "That was the witch's fault. Morgawse. She was supposed to hold it stable. You must have scared her off, barging in, interfering."

I snorted. "She was long gone before we arrived. Morgan's gone to chase her down. You were in over your head, Michel. The fact you counted on Morgawse proves that. She only does what benefits her. My guess, she wanted to siphon the energy from the implosion of the netherworlds, before she 'stabilized' anything. She tried something similar before." I tested my limbs by taking a step forward. I didn't fall, so I moved in closer. "Either that or she saw her chance to abandon you and escape, assuming you'd be trapped when the netherworlds imploded."

"If that's true, she'll pay." Nostradamus straightened his spine, edging backward. "But it worked. The darkness has been contained for now. My plan worked."

"Bollocks!" I moved forward, my anger building. "You're lucky I bailed your sorry arse from catastrophe! And you weren't containing anything, you greedy bastard. I saw what you did, siphoning off the power for yourself. You could have cycled it back into the realms and lowered the risk. It would have better prevented the spread of the dark magicks as well, by cutting the realm from the weave of the energy. Your plan was reckless!"

"How dare you!"

His hand slashed upward and a flash of light

blinded me. Energy shot out of his fingertips and a discharge of magic slammed me in the chest. I went down, landing on my back in a haze of sound, sizzle, and knocked-about senses. I groaned, my ears ringing, my head pounding, my chest burning in a bone-jarring ache. Shadows shifted in my double vision and I heard footsteps. I scrambled to my knees as Nostradamus escaped through a portal.

I spat again, a little blood in the spittle, and swore. I got to my feet, knees shaking and stumbled out of the grotto. I lurched down the corridor and as I turned a corner I ran into Morgan and Vivienne.

"You look like shit!" Morgan's voice greeted me. "What happened?"

"I stopped the realms from imploding, but Nostradamus got away."

Morgan scowled. "So did Morgawse. She had a portal ready and waiting and an anti-tracking spell. The bitch. We decided to come back for you when the shaking stopped."

I cradled my side, wincing with pain.

"Can you get us the hell out of here, Viv?"

She nodded.

"Good. Then let's go home."

Chapter Nine

Merlin

I sat in the garden, watching the sunrise, drinking tea and wishing it was whisky. I heard footsteps and then Morgan's voice.

"You're up early."

I glanced back. She was already dressed for the day. "I didn't sleep well after yesterday. Why are you up?"

"The same." She crossed in front of me and sat in another chair. "I gave up around five AM." She sighed. "We're in a mess, aren't we?"

"That we are. Do you want a cup of tea? I can fetch one from the kitchen."

"No. What I want is something stronger but it's

too early in the morning." She kicked a pebble. "I had two chances, two. And I blew it both times. I don't know what I'm going to do about my sister. All I know is she can't remain free. She's too dangerous."

I nodded. "Nostradamus is out of control too. His behaviour yesterday..." I shook my head. "He nearly destroyed a netherworld and he didn't have to. He did it for the power; I could see it in his eyes." I sipped my tea. "I don't think we can trust him to fix this, and we certainly can't trust him with Merlin's grimoire." I put my cup down. "As much as I hate to say this, we are going to have to find the grimoire first and make sure he never gets his hands on it."

"And when we do," Morgan asked, "will you try to reverse the spell? Are you going to save magic?"

"I don't know." I blew out a breath of air and exasperation. "Everything's a jumbled mess. Immortality is a bitch and you know it, but losing magic..." I paused, biting at my lip. "That's more complicated and involves so much. I'm not sure I'm the right person to make the decision. Or if I have the right to make the decision."

"Someone thinks you have the right," Morgan

grunted. "Gwenevere for one. Mark for another. This mysterious Lady. And maybe even the Daughters of Avalon. Every bloody mysterious entity pulling strings in this game seems to be pushing you towards fixing this mess. Or letting it happen. Or something. I say we just get the book and figure it out from there."

I snickered. "You just want to look at Merlin's grimoire."

"Maybe I do. What's wrong with that?" She shrugged. "Question is, how are we going to find it? You heard Iseult, she isn't going anywhere near Mark. And I doubt he'll give up the key without her. Whatever this key is. And even if we do get it, how do we get to Annwn?" She tapped her fingers on the arm of her chair. "The Tylwyth Teg aren't inclined to welcome visitors."

"No idea." I shrugged and finished the last of the tea in my cup. Then a banging came from the kitchen, followed by a yelp from Martin.

"I'll go." Morgan pushed herself up from her chair. "See what the little twit is up to and if he's making breakfast again."

Morgan's footsteps echoed into the morning

tranquility as she walked into the house. I settled back in my chair and closed my eyes.

I listened to the flutter of leaves in the wind, breathed in the smell of the roses, and heard the chirping of the birds. My mind drifted along the channels of nature, feeling the power underneath it, spreading across the earth. There was a joy of life there, mixed within the soil, sprouting in the grass, wafting along currents of air into the sky, among the clouds and finally out into the cosmos. It was peaceful and I let myself float with the energy.

I'll miss this if magic dies.

I might have stayed there all morning if something hadn't called my name.

Nimue.

I opened my eyes. No one was in the garden with me. My skin shivered.

Destiny will find you. You travel the lines of fate.

I jumped to my feet and looked around. Not a soul in the garden. No sign of magic. No hint of a spell. Just the voice.

He's found a way. He's coming tonight. Ward the garden.

Don't let its secret escape. Not yet.

And then there was silence. No sound of wind or birds or anything. It felt like the garden had dropped into a void. The temperature lowered and I shivered with the chill. I backed away a few steps, looking over my shoulder at the door to the cottage. I thought about running but then the voice spoke one last time.

Make your choices. Turn the wheel. Destiny's coming for you.

I SPENT the rest of the day locked in my shed preparing spelled warding and protections and then setting it all properly within the garden. I was ready to defend my home against any kind of threat I could imagine and then some. I exhausted my supply of amber for a special shielding spell and prepared a nasty surprise with a piece of agate carved in runes. When a mysterious voice tells you there's a threat on the way, you pay attention.

I had a pretty good idea the threat I faced was from Nostradamus, but why he thought to make a move against me I couldn't fathom. The only reason to come was if he wanted something. But he knew I didn't have the grimoire, so why? It didn't make sense. Yet, I couldn't take any chances. If that whacked-out wizard was coming, I'd give him one hell of a reception.

With the last ward in place—a special surprise I conjured from portal dust and a spell I had acquired from an Italian witch—I looked everything over to make sure I hadn't forgotten anything or made a mistake. Satisfied everything was in order, I went inside the cottage and poured myself a glass of wine. The only thing left was to wait until sunset.

Morgan soon joined me and poured herself a glass of wine as well. "So, we're up against it again. What do you think the blighter wants?"

"No idea. I guess we'll find out later." I took a sip of wine. We were both avoiding the real issue, the mysterious person behind the message. "So where are Iseult and Martin? And Vivienne?"

"Hiding upstairs, I think. At least Martin and Iseult are. I think they're both panicked by all this. Last I saw Vivienne, she was cross-legged on a bed in a guest bedroom chanting. I assume she's still there, but haven't got a clue what she's doing."

"Best not ask. Especially if she's in one of her trances. We will find out eventually. I just hope it doesn't involve screaming; I've had enough of that lately." I drank more wine as Morgan chuckled.

"So, you think this protection you've installed in the garden will hold off Nostradamus? Or are we going to go toe-to-toe with that wizard?" Morgan swirled the wine in her glass before taking a sip.

"Only time will tell. It should at least curtail his magic, though. I just wish I knew why he was coming. What does he want?"

"Yeah. And why the garden? What's out there that's so special?" Morgan nearly spilled her wine as we both realized what Nostradamus was after.

Together we exclaimed, "Merlin!"

I added, "That's what she meant, 'he's found a way'. Nostradamus has found a way to free Merlin. The bastard. The bloody bastard."

Morgan's hand shook and she set down her glass

of wine. "You can stop him, though, right? Merlin won't go free?"

My stomach did flip-flops. What sort of spell had Nostradamus conjured that could break the transformation I had laid on Merlin? That was earth magic, a rite bound to the sacred power of Samhain. It would take a lot of strength to break that spell. Was that the real reason he had drained the energy from the Netherworld? To have enough power to free Merlin? To turn him back into flesh and blood?

"Damn, I hope not. The combination of Nostradamus *and* Merlin scares the crap out of me."

Morgan shivered. "Don't forget Morgawse. I don't fancy our odds against those three."

"Agreed." I swallowed the last of my wine, emptying my glass, and poured myself another. "But you know what this means, don't you?" Morgan shook her head. "It means, I'm bloody going to have to defend Merlin and save the bastard from Nostradamus." I drained my second glass of wine and filled the glass again. "It's total bollocks."

AGAINST THE setting rays of the sun and the first shades of twilight, Morgan and I waited in the garden for signs of Nostradamus' predicted incursion. Iseult and Martin stayed in the parlour as our emergency backup. The way they whined I hoped to hell we wouldn't need them. Vivienne was still upstairs, lost in her own private inner space.

We didn't have long to wait. With a faint crackle and hum evocative of electricity, a portal rift opened in the field adjacent to my cottage and two figures emerged past the magic and shadows. I took a breath, clenching the little gift I had prepared for my old friends. I wondered which one would receive it.

"Good thing my neighbours aren't the nosey sort," I mumbled.

My fingers itched as the pair walked slowly towards us. The back gate creaked as they entered, and their footsteps trod loudly down the path.

"Hello, Michel, Morgawse." My gaze lingered on her. Her eyes were bloodshot and her cheek looked bruised. She was limping, and she looked like she was in pain. I looked sharply at Nostradamus but said nothing.

He tilted his head, lifting his chin. "We have come for—"

"Bollocks on the speeches, we already figured it out. You're after Merlin."

Nostradamus sputtered at my interruption and Morgawse snickered.

I scowled. "Turn around and head back, if you know what's good for you. Merlin stays the way he is and you won't be transforming that arsehole back."

Morgawse edged around Nostradamus and closer to Morgan. "I told you she'd say that."

"What she says or wants means nothing. We will have Merlin."

"That's why I prepared for guests." I tossed my little agate surprise at Nostradamus hitting him square in the chest. It exploded in a burst of energy and satisfying payback that rocked him on his heels.

He laughed as he tried to dust powered agate from his clothes. "Is that the best you can do? Pitiful."

I smiled. "Wait for it."

As the words left my mouth, the spell's secondary

after effect kicked in and Nostradamus lit up in a barrage of lightning that would do Thor proud. My magic knocked a screaming Nostradamus on his keister as his flesh and clothing seared and his body shuddered from the electricity. Before I could move in to finish him, movement to my right caught my attention. Morgan and Morgawse.

The two sisters rushed each other, screeching, and the garden blazed in magical energy. I ducked to avoid their carelessly flung power and Nostradamus rolled through my tulip patch to douse the lightning still snapping at him. Above it all, came squealing insults.

"Bitch!"

"Hag!"

More shrieks and insults followed, as the sisters conjured energy balls that they slammed into each other. Evenly matched, they went hand-to-hand in a knockdown, drag-out brawl. They struggled and wrestled, stumbling across the garden.

Shit. They were too close to the hydrangeas.

"Morgan, watch out!" I shouted but it was too late. She and Morgawse stumbled over the ward and triggered it. The magic flashed, and in an instant, both were transported away.

"Shit!" But Morgan was gone. At least Morgawse went with her. I hoped they wouldn't be too pissed off at landing in Wales.

"Now it's just you and me, old friend."

I looked at Michel—no, this wasn't my Michel—this was Nostradamus. He stood on shaky legs; burned, furious, and smelling of ozone and smoke.

He straightened his shoulders and dusted off his clothes. "Just let me do what must be done; let me cast the spell. Let me restore Merlin and take him away. Together we will fix magic and return the world to the way it was."

I looked at him, standing there so proud, so arrogant, even streaked in electrical burns. For a moment, so reminiscent of Merlin. Any residual feeling I had melted away. I circled him, putting myself between him and the tree he wanted to restore back into a pompous prick of a wizard.

"Not a chance. If you want Merlin, you go through me."

"So be it." He inhaled, winced, and then chanted spell words. His hands flashed with energy.

I took one step back. I felt my foot hit the prepared stone and the garden lit up like a Christmas tree; every ward, every charm, every protection spell went active.

My lips twitched as I repressed the urge to cackle. "Merlin made the same mistake. He underestimated me too."

Only then did Nostradamus realize what I had done but he couldn't stop the spell. Instead of hitting its target, namely me, it backfired directly into him.

The resulting shockwave levitated him upward, and for some reason, sideways. He flew over the back fence and landed smack dab in the middle of a bramble bush. Stifling my laughter, I raced after him.

# Chapter Ten

At Odds

As I ran through the back gate, I saw Nostradamus arse over kettle, feet sticking to the sky in the middle of the brambles. He squirmed there for some seconds before he crawled out of the bushes. The moment he freed himself, I slammed an energy ball across the air and into his chest, knocking him back on his pins. He rolled along the grass, with a delightful scream, as I threw more magical energy. I bombarded him with repeated hits until he was unconscious and sprawled over charred grass.

I stood over his inert form, my breath heaving from exertion, power sparking off my fingertips. "Nobody messes with Merlin, you bloody bastard!" As I stared, letting the adrenaline and anger dissipate, I realized I had a bigger problem. "Oh, shit! What the hell am I going to do with him now?"

I gave him a kick to make sure he was well and truly out of it and took a breath. I connected with the flow and shift of magic, and whispered, "*Cydi a arnifyo.*"

Nostradamus quivered, his limbs twitching; he slowly rose until I had the fool hovering a few feet off the ground. I flicked my wrist and the levitation spell responded, jerking him a few feet forward, in the direction of the cottage. 1 then walked back home trailing his unconscious body behind me. Iseult and Martin raced out into the garden as I dumped Nostradamus on the paving stones near the roses, flat on his back.

"Is he dead?" Martin's fearful voice spoke first.

"Of course not, silly," Iseult replied before I had a chance. "He's immortal, like the rest of us. Looks like he got knocked around, though. That'll sting when he wakes up."

I raised an eyebrow but only said, "Watch him, will you? I need to fetch something. Hit him with a jolt of energy if he stirs."

Iseult nodded and I left her and Martin standing guard while I went around the cottage. I hastened into my shed, pushing some storage crates around, before grabbing an old tin box. Then I headed back to the garden.

Martin and Iseult were now seated, watching the still form of Nostradamus. I walked over and beckoned to Martin. "Help me turn him over on his stomach."

Martin hesitated, but only for a second. He joined me and we knelt down beside the insensible wizard. Then we turned Nostradamus over to flop down on his face. I set the box down and took out a pair of rune-inscribed shackles.

Iseult gave a gentle gasp. "Are those binding runes? Are you going to fetter his magic?"

"Yes, and yes." Pulling his arms back, I snapped the bonds over Nostradamus' wrists. The metal glowed briefly, as the magic activated, and the runes shimmered in a soft blue light. "There, that should keep him out of trouble until we can figure out what to bloody well do next." I stood, motioning for Martin to move back, and flexed my wrist. Nostradamus rose on the levitation spell and hovered.

Martin piped up, "What are you going to do with him?"

"Stick him in cold storage in the shed for a bit. I need to figure out what's going on before coming up with a permanent fix for the prat."

I moved forward and Nostradamus followed like an obedient puppy. Iseult and Martin trailed after us and we all traipsed out into the shed. I dropped Nostradamus against the back wall and then rummaged about in my storage boxes scraping enough ingredients together to make a small amount of protection powder.

This won't be enough, unless…

"Go fetch half a dozen wards from the garden," I snapped at Martin, who jumped and dashed off. "And be careful, they're still active." I turned to Iseult. "Fetch me the mortar and pestle off the shelf will you?"

As she retrieved the implements, I sorted the substances and found my measuring spoon. I doled out the bay leaves, salt, lavender, and eggshells before grinding the combination into a fine powder. I added two sprigs of cedar wood, a dollop of rose thorns and crushed it all together. Finally, I mixed in a drop of frankincense oil and dumped the final product in a glass jar. Martin rushed back into the shed as I put away the mortar and pestle.

He handed me the wards and I noticed his fingers were singed. "I told you to be careful." He shrugged and I shook my head.

I placed the wards in a circle around Nostradamus and sprinkled a line of powder to join each ward together. Then I stepped back with an empty jar and spoke the spell. "*Seliwchy gyfodclo wech ydrwys. Cadwchyr hynydd ytu mywn bythby thoedd cyrchyr.*"

As I said the last word of the incantation, Nostradamus let out a groan and the magic shielding activated to imprison him behind a barrier of blue energy. It pulsed for a moment before fading to a transparent sheen in the air.

Martin exclaimed, "I think he's waking up."

"Good." I slipped another thing I had gathered—a protection amulet—around my neck. "I want a word or two with him." I glanced at the pair. "Alone." At their frowns, I added, "You two head back inside. Keep an eye out for more trouble. Morgawse may come back. And check on Vivienne. I think she's stopped chanting."

Iseult and Martin headed out, a bit reluctantly I thought, which was nice. Maybe they were finally settling into the reality of it all.

I turned my attention back to Nostradamus.

His eyelids fluttered and he emitted another groan. His leg twitched and his eyes opened slowly. He looked at me, dazed, until recognition finally dawned. He snarled, moving his hands, suddenly realizing they were shackled. He tried to scramble to his feet, still shaky, leaning against the wall and stumbling, until he rose to his full height. Then he rushed at me.

And ran smack into the magical barrier keeping him imprisoned. It knocked him back on his bum and he skidded across the concrete floor until he hit the wall.

"What have you done?" He shouted, his voice dripping in fury, arrogance, and indignation.

"Just rendered you harmless for the time being. I can't have you running around willy-nilly doing whatever you want and causing trouble. Like trying to free psycho wizards. You've gone rogue, Michel, and I can't have it." I looked at him in disappointment and disgust.

He grimaced. "You have no idea what you've done. What will happen. I'm the only one that can stop it. The only one that can save the world."

"Listen to yourself; you sound barmy. You might be powerful, but you're not the magical Messiah." I shook my head. "You let your ego get the better of you. You aren't thinking of the consequences, what comes next even if you save magic. You're being reckless. Too reckless to ignore or to let roam free. You're going to cool your heels in my shed until I can find a more permanent solution for you. Maybe a little time alone will give you some perspective. You need it."

His face morphed into an expression of hurt like he was a puppy I'd just whipped.

I snorted. "Don't give me that hangdog look. You came into my home, tried to restore Merlin and send him back out into the world. What were you thinking? Merlin's dangerous. You may have new skills and power but you can't handle *him*."

He sneered. "Don't judge me on your inability to handle him."

"Fuck, you're a tosser." I wanted to reach through

the barrier and punch him. "Did you think he'd be grateful if you freed him and you'd be best mates? That he'd fall in line and help you? More likely he'd have banished you to a netherworld hell and done the job himself. And then the rest of us would be left to clean up the mess." I snorted. "Why don't you start using that vaunted brain of yours to actually do something sensible?"

"And what is your solution? Ignore the problem? You cannot fight this without me. Let me out of this prison."

I stood there, watching him glower, his back pressed up against the wall, leaning against his shackled arms.

"No, you stay put. You're a danger. Dangerous people get imprisoned." I turned on my heel, walked away, and left the shed.

THE HOUSE and garden were quiet, and thankfully no neighbours were banging on the door from the ruckus. I guess after these many years they'd learned to ignore the odd happenings. Voices resonated from upstairs and I went to investigate. I peeked around Vivienne's open door and didn't see anyone, but noises were emanating from the loo. I walked into the room to witness the spectacle of Vivienne hanging over the toilet with Iseult holding her hair back and Martin staring at the wall. Vivienne retched and I looked away. A few moments later, Martin rushed past me. His footsteps thumped downstairs.

"Vivienne's visions make her ill again?" I asked. "I keep something for her stomach troubles in the cupboard by the sink. The blue bottle."

I heard rummaging noises, more gagging and then silence. Then the flush of the toilet. I turned back. Iseult assisted Vivienne to her feet and then to the bed, where she helped Vivienne to lie down. Viv closed her eyes and Iseult moved away to sit in a nearby chair.

I watched Iseult, who stared at Vivienne with a worried expression. "It must have been a tough one if it hit her this hard. The aftereffects aren't usually this bad."

"I think she may have encountered some of the dark magic. At one point, before the fight in the garden, her eyes went black for a few seconds." Iseult shot me a worried look. "The corruption is still spreading. I tried a scrying spell earlier, and it fizzled out in a spray of inky sparks."

"Damn. I was hoping that netherworld stunt would have slowed it down more." I glanced back at Viv, who seemed to be falling asleep. "Did she say anything?"

"Only bits and pieces, jumbles really. Nothing that made much sense." Iseult sighed. "Things about glass and castles. Spells and gardens. And darkness. It was confusing and quite frightening. I hope she is more coherent later."

"She should be. Let her sleep." I reached over and pulled a blanket over Vivienne. "I've done this before. She needs rest. Come downstairs. I could use your help finding Morgan."

Iseult glanced up at me. "Morgan's missing? I thought she went chasing after Morgawse. I mean, after they weren't there. In the garden. When…" She stumbled over her words, looking a bit guilty.

I felt a twinge of guilt of my own. "She, um, accidentally tripped one of the wards. It sent her and Morgawse to Wales."

"Wales?"

"A small cabin near Mount Snowdon to be precise.

We should probably check on her."

Iseult put a hand over her mouth trying to stifle a giggle, but the laughter tumbled out. "Morgan in rural Wales? Oh, the poor Welsh." More laughter spilled from her lips and I chuckled with her.

"Come on." I tilted my head towards the bedroom door. "Let's go save the Welsh from the wrath of Morgan."

MORGAN STEPPED through the portal into the garden and scowled at me. In the glow of the hanging lights, she looked as if misery spat on her, and she smelled like she had slept in week-old rubbish. I took a step backward as the magic faded, covering my nose with my hand and trying not to gag. Her clothes and hair were caked in some kind of mud that flaked off when she moved, repeatedly wafting her stench into the air.

I moved farther back, my stomach churning. "What happened to you?"

"Bloody Wales is what happened!" She snapped, her whole body seething. "And a bloody bog! I fell into a bloody bog! And Morgawse escaped again!" She flounced down into a chair, in a spray of dried mud and stink. I eyed the garden hose and considered giving her a good rinse.

"That doesn't sound pleasant," I remarked, still eying the hose.

"Of course, it wasn't," she retorted, "and I nearly got arrested." She scowled at me again. "At least tell me you stopped that other tosser, Nostradamus."

I nodded. "He's locked up in the shed."

"In the shed?" She looked at me with astonishment. "Oh, hell. I don't want to know. Just get me a damned whisky."

I left and fetched a bottle and two glasses, plus some air freshener. I dumped some artificial scent in the air to counteract Welsh bog and then poured two whiskies. I gingerly handed Morgan her glass and then sat as far away, and as downwind, as possible.

"Tell me about Morgawse."

She growled. "The fucking bitch ran as soon as we landed in Wales. She conked me one and did a runner. I gave chase and we spent the bloody evening dashing over half of Wales it seemed like, magic skirmishes across the damned countryside." She sipped some whisky. "Probably inspired a few more bloody legends while we were at it." She drank some more and added, "That's how I ended up in the bog. Least I pulled the hag in with me."

I hid my amusement over those two wrestling in a bog. "So is that where you lost her?"

Morgan stared into her glass. The muscles in her jaw tightened. "I don't know how she escaped. One minute we were crawling out of the muck and the next… she started glowing and swearing and then she was gone. It looked a bit like portal energy but… I don't know. It wasn't any magic I'd seen before." She swallowed some more whisky. "But it whisked her away, whatever it was, and the bitch is still free."

I rubbed a finger around the rim of my glass. Morgan's words tickled a memory loose from the back of my mind. "Maybe not as free as you might think."

Morgan cast me a sharp glance. "What do you mean? Do you know something?"

"Maybe. What you described sounded familiar. And something Nostradamus said at our first meeting in the garden. That he could fetch Morgawse back when he needed."

I swirled my whisky and took a sip. The alcohol stung my throat and I savoured the taste and feeling. "Nostradamus may have laid a retrieval spell on her."

At Morgan's confused look I explained further. "It's an obscure variant on those fucking slave collar spells, and a nasty piece of spell work, very intricate and hard to get right. That's why most wizards and witches don't use it. If you get it wrong bad things happen." I swallowed more whisky. "I've only seen it twice in my lifetimes. Once successfully, the other time…" I shuddered. "Well, it involved a lot of blood and brain matter."

"What exactly does it do?" Morgan asked, with a trace of worry in her voice.

"You weave the spell into a practitioner's essence and bind them to restrict their freedom. They're restrained from straying beyond the boundaries and time limits set by the caster. Depending on the specifics of the spell, the magic can be attached to the spellcaster or a place, and will 'retrieve' them if they try to break their bindings." I looked down, avoiding Morgan's increasingly shocked gaze. "And since she didn't end up in my shed, I'm guessing when Morgawse triggered the spell, she was retrieved to wherever

Nostradamus was calling home."

"Then that bastard knows exactly where she is." Morgan placed her empty glass on the paving stones, beside a leg of her chair. "Let's go ask him, so she and I can settle things once and for all. Then she can be safely tucked back into a sleeping beauty prison where she belongs."

"We can do that," I agreed, "but first, you take a shower. Or I'll hose you off here. You reek of bog and it's a powerful stench."

Morgan glanced down at herself, dusting some of the mud off her clothes. "I suppose I do need a shower and a change of clothes. There is a rather strong pong, isn't there."

She stood and I ushered her into the cottage to the downstairs bathroom so she could clean up. I laid out some clothes for her to change into and some towels and then I went back to the garden. I collected the whisky glasses, then hosed down her chair and the area around it. After I was through, I went back inside to wait for her. Thirty minutes later she emerged from the bathroom, wearing clean clothes and a towel wrapped around her wet hair.

"Let's go find out where Morgawse is stashed." She

marched in the direction of the shed without waiting for an answer; I scrambled to keep up. She didn't pause or hesitate until she was inside face-to-face with Nostradamus.

"Where's my sister, you old coot? Tell me so I can kick her ass back into hibernation oblivion where she belongs."

Nostradamus jerked his head up and stiffened. "How dare you speak to me that way!"

She straightened her spine and with her most haughty voice she shouted, "I'm Morgan le Fay and I can speak to you any bloody way I please!" Magical energy snapped off her fingers. "Now answer the question, you faffing French twat!"

The look on his face was priceless, a mix of outrage, fear and awe, and I couldn't help chuckling.

Nostradamus looked at me and then back at Morgan. He slumped his shoulders. "I can tell you where she is."

That was too quick. What's he up to?

Then he grinned. "But her location will do you no good, for you cannot travel there. Only Morgawse or I may enter. I am not so much," he paused, then added, "a faffing fool to leave my sanctuary or her unsecured. And as long as I am here she can rot in her little prison." He chuckled. "Or you can let me out and I will bring her here. An even trade. Morgawse for my freedom."

"Bollocks to that!" Morgan glared, and her fingers curled into fists. "I say we turn him into a frog and use him as a rugby ball until he tells us how to get to her. Or brings her here." Real fear blossomed in his eyes as she advanced. "Or maybe just some old-fashioned torture. I haven't pulled off anyone's ears in ages. I bet you cave after twenty minutes of pain."

"I'd say less than that." I chimed in, enjoying Nostradamus' discomfort. "He's soft. Chop off his fingers and when they grow back, chop them off again. That'll loosen his tongue."

"Oh, good one." Morgan's face lit up at the prospect. "Maybe we could actually loosen his tongue and yank it out of his mouth." She gave Nostradamus a very unsettling stare. "He talks too much anyway."

Nostradamus backed away from her, scurrying like a rat. "You, madame, are insane." He turned to me. "You would not allow her to commit such atrocities against me, would you?"

I shrugged. "Morgan generally does as she pleases. And I generally don't get in her way."

"Bah. I do not believe you. You would not let me suffer."

I shrugged again, and said, "He's all yours, Morgan." I took a few steps towards the door.

"Wait!"

I stopped at the sound of his shout, turning back.

"What you want cannot be done without my magic." He paused, twitching, as Morgan made a noise very much like a snarl of a wild animal. "But I will tell you where she is located. Then you will see."

"That works for me," I replied. "For now." I looked over at Morgan who glanced between us.

"Fine." She clenched her jaw. "But I reserve the right to pull off this wanker's ears."

I nodded. Then I asked a slightly outraged Nostradamus, "Where is she?"

Nostradamus leaned against the wall, cocking his head. "She is in Joyeuse Garde."

"Shit!" I glared at him as he laughed, before

turning tail and marching outside. A swearing Morgan followed me.

Chapter Eleven

Escapes and Visions

"Bloody, no good bastard. The bloody bastard. Of the rotten, thieving things to do." I mumbled and paced in the parlour until Morgan yelled at me.

"What are you going on about? Joyeuse Garde is from one of those ridiculous legends. Something to do with Lancelot, I remember that. We just ask Lance which one of his blasted places ended up with that name and grab my sister out of there. Easy peasy."

I stared for a minute as her words penetrated past my funk and into my brain. Then I snapped, "Not that Joyeuse Garde. The one I created. Or almost created. The one that bounder stole for himself!"

Morgan tilted her head. "What the bloody hell are you going on about? What do you mean, you created? He stole?"

I fidgeted. "It was just supposed to be an idea. A thought experiment. A wish, an idle notion. It wasn't supposed to be real. But he made it real. He took it from me."

Morgan tapped her foot and exclaimed in exasperation. "You had better start explaining yourself. Now."

"It was an idea to create a hidden pocket inside a netherworld, an escape. A place to get away from the world. I called it Joyeuse Garde as a joke. But it was a fantasy, it was never supposed to become reality."

"And I take it you told Nostradamus about this?"

I nodded.

"So this ex of yours appropriated your idea and created it? Created this pocket dimension within an existing netherworld." Morgan shook her head. "He is a prat. But if it was your idea doesn't that mean that there might be a way for you to access it? Get Morgawse out?"

This time I shook my head. "I doubt it. If he used my original design, then it can only be entered by people who have been granted access. But," I frowned, thinking, "we might be able to spy on it. At least see where she is and how she is doing."

"At least that's something. We could give it a shot." Morgan flopped down in a chair.

"Yeah, we could, we…" A knock at the parlour door interrupted my thought.

The door opened before I could answer and Iseult popped her head in. "I think you two better come upstairs. Vivienne's awake. She wants to talk to you."

"Great. Now what?" I exhaled and followed Iseult back upstairs, Morgan trailing the both of us. We all went into Vivienne's bedroom.

She sat on the bed, waiting for us. Martin stood in the corner looking scared. Viv waved her hand, motioning for us to sit. When we had our bums down in chairs she gave us a solemn look and took a breath.

"As you know, I went on a vision quest yesterday and much was revealed to me. It's all very strange and peculiar, and I'm not sure I understand it all, but there are things that have to be said and you have to be told."

She looked down in her lap and fidgeted with her hands, plucking at the cloth of her skirt. "First, Nostradamus is right. The corruption caused by the blood sacrifice spell must be contained or reversed. Magic cannot fall to the darkness, or consequences beyond imaging will happen. Irrevocable and ancient consequences." She looked at me and repeated, "It has to be stopped." And then she added, "And no matter what happens, I believe immortality will remain. You cannot change that fate."

I looked down, my heart breaking a little. *I knew it was too good to be true.*

Morgan broke into the conversation, "So are you saying we have to let the wanker in the shed go, and let him fix this?"

Vivienne smoothed the bedspread with her hand and shook her head. "Nostradamus can't be the one. He has his role to play, but not that. The balance of magic is being shifted and Nostradamus is not the one to accomplish what must be done."

She looked at me and then looked away and then looked at me again. Written on her face was a swirl of hope, fear and sorrow. "Nimue is the one that has to do it." She spat out the high-pitched words. "And you're going to need Merlin's grimoire. You're going to have to travel to Tintagel and see Mark." She then turned towards Iseult, speaking softly, but firmly. "And I'm afraid you're going to have to go with her."

Iseult's screech shook the bedroom window panes.

"Shut up!" Vivienne's barking order silenced the room. Iseult glared at her, and Viv glowered back. I kept my mouth closed. I knew what was coming and knew better than to interfere. I noticed Morgan stayed quiet as well, and Martin tried to shrink into the wallpaper.

"I don't want to hear it!" Vivienne jumped off the bed and towered over a now frightened Iseult. "No excuses. You are going! This is too important, and I will not let your selfish, petty feuds interfere. You will face Mark and you will resolve this issue that has been going on for centuries. No more running. No more hiding. You will step up and do what must be done."

"But, but... I..." Iseult stammered, unable to get out a coherent objection under Vivienne's stare. I couldn't blame her. The formidable side of Vivienne could wilt the strongest soul.

"I don't want to hear it!" she commanded. "You are going to Tintagel with Nimue. We all are." She whirled on Morgan and Martin who quickly nodded in agreement.

"Good. Then everyone get out except Nimue. We still need to talk."

The other three tripped over their feet to leave and I was alone with Vivienne.

She paced the floor for a bit before getting to the point. Then she stopped and stared at the carving on the bed's footboard. She wouldn't look me in the eye as she spoke.

"There's a darkness underneath all this. Something very old. I could feel it waiting in the shadows as I travelled through the netherworlds, waiting on the edges of my vision. Something hateful, and powerful." She shivered.

I frowned, confused. "Are you talking about that dark wizard? The wanker that started all this?"

"No. Not him, though I sensed he is bound up in this too." She glanced at me. "He may be as much a pawn in this as we are. There's something else happening. Didn't you feel it when you connected to Stonehenge?"

I shifted in my chair and looked at the floor. "Maybe." Then I lifted my chin. "What does any of it have to do with me?"

"It all has to do with you. You're the only thing standing between this creature and his goal. That's why you need the grimoire. If you have that you may be able to stop him. Certainly, you can stop what's happening now. I saw that clearly." Vivienne sat back down on the bed.

"Bollocks! You got it wrong, Viv." Irritation and fear prickled against my words. "You're talking like I was some kind of mystic saviour from a crap TV show. You're better off with Nostradamus. I don't trust him anymore but he's more powerful, and capable. And he actually wants to save magic." I kicked at the carpet as my frustration boiled over.

Vivienne glared at me, and I squirmed under her disapproval.

But I didn't give in. "If we just explain what's truly going on, Michel can do it. I say we put him on a leash and let him have at it. Let him use the grimoire and unspell what's been done. I can keep the damn book afterwards if I need to. I wouldn't want it in his hands anyway."

I bit my lip, staring back down at the floor. "It doesn't have to be me. It doesn't have to be. Why am I the one that has to undo this blood sacrifice, malevolent magic bollocks? Or deal with ancient whatevers?"

"If Nostradamus is the one, the future…" Vivienne's body suddenly stiffened, and she turned to me, her eyes white and glowing. Her voice deepened as she spoke.

"If the hand of the prophet wields the blade to bind the wounds, destiny will fall. Darkness will call the darkness. The threads that weave us all together will fray and crack and blacken. Doom will descend upon us all."

For a few moments there was only the sound of her breathing, and then her voice hissed, "He will force the choice and feed the darkness. Only the one who fights her destiny will be the one to restore the balance." Vivienne raised her hand and pointed at me. "You are the one. The only one." Then she lowered her hand, her body relaxed and her eyes returned to normal.

"Bollocks!" I jumped from my chair and glared at Vivienne. "Double bollocks!"

Vivienne reached out and rubbed my shoulder. "I'm sorry. It's just the way it has to be."

"Typical. I'm knee-deep in someone else's mess whether I want to be or not. How the bloody hell did I get designated the bloody go to, fix-it gal? If I ever get a hold of any of these fucking mysterious types floating around behind the scenes, I'm going to give them a piece of my bloody mind!"

"So you'll do it? You'll find the grimoire and undo the blood sacrifice spell?"

"No one's leaving me a choice in the matter, are they? Not with bloody doom hanging over our heads." I scowled. "I'm getting tired of bloody doom. And wankers messing with things that should be left alone. I swear, the next arsehole who decides they want to muck around in some magic powerplay is going to end up living the rest of their immortal life as a toad by your lake, Viv."

She chuckled. "Nice to know you're taking it so well."

"How am I supposed to take being appointed the saviour of the fucking world?"

"Don't get angry at me." Viv pouted. "I'm sorry I'm the

messenger, but this is serious. That other... thing out there." She shivered again. "There's only one word for it. Evil. I've never felt anything like it. The hate. The malevolence. And so very old. Waiting, growing, getting more and more powerful. He—it hates. A pure visceral hate."

I frowned, catching Vivienne's odd use of pronouns. "Is this presence an 'it' or a 'he'?"

"Both, neither. I'm not sure. I sensed two different entities, but entwined together. I don't know. Maybe one was your wizard. Things, sights, feelings shifted too much, like sand and water through my fingers." She furrowed her brow. "I felt a living hate and then what seemed like a living shadow. Thoughts with no substance and then a storm that surrounded you."

"Fucking perfect."

Vivienne scowled and stuck out her tongue. Then she tilted her head, a slight glow around her eyes. She hummed slightly and asked, "Did you invite Morgawse to tea? She's here for a visit. Downstairs, downstairs. To set the seer free."

"Shit!" I raced from the bedroom, shouting as I ran, "Morgawse is in the shed!"

Everyone lurking outside in the hallway yelped and Morgan swore as we all dashed outside and burst into the shed. But we were too late. Morgawse was standing inside the barrier I had spelled, beside Nostradamus. His shackles lay on the floor by his feet. I ground my teeth as I watched him bow his head and flourish his hand, all while leaning on Morgawse. And then they were gone; a portal opened and swallowed them.

"Damnation!" I spat on the ground.

Beside me, Morgan cursed, "Bloody hell!" and slammed her fist against a crate.

Martin exclaimed, "What just happened?"

"I got sloppy," I replied. "Underestimated that bastard. And now he's free. Damn it! Damn it all to hell!"

"But how?" Iseult's bewildered voice broke in. "How did she break your spell?"

"She didn't." I still felt my magic, intact and untampered. "My guess, it was the bloody retrieval spell. He called her to him. I should have thought of that. Now they're both free again." I wanted to punch something. "Shit!"

"At least they don't know where the grimoire is."

Martin chimed in again, trying to sound positive.

"Um," Morgan's voice interrupted. "That's not quite true. I might have let it slip to Morgawse that Mark knows where the book is located."

"What?" My urge to punch something shifted to Morgan but I restrained myself. "You told Morgawse Mark has Merlin's grimoire?"

"Yes. I didn't mean to, it just came out when we were arguing, in the heat of the moment. But they don't know where Mark is, so maybe we go after Morgawse and Nostradamus directly. Track them down before they figure out his whereabouts."

I glared. "Sure I could track them down, they probably headed straight back to Joyeuse Garde to regroup. But we still can't enter, so what good..." I stopped mid-sentence, an idea suddenly occurring to me. "We can't enter but maybe we can fix it so they can't leave. At least temporarily. Slow them down so we can get ahead of them." I looked at their confused—and in Morgan's case, guilty—faces and tried not to grind my teeth. "Come on, I'll need everyone's help with this and then we can leave for Tintagel and confront Mark."

Chapter Twelve

Tintagel

We pushed back the furniture and cleared space on the floor in my back office. I laid out a loose circle of quartz and citrine crystals inscribed with symbols of my own design. Within that, I fashioned a smaller circle of wooden Norse runes. Morgan, Vivienne, Iseult, and Martin stood at equal distance points along the edge of the outer circle and I stood in the center of the inner one. In turn, I faced the others, spoke the spell word to connect them to the magic and wove them into the enchantment.

"*Nytaff.*" Morgan connected to the spell.

"*Chwradd.*" I brought in Iseult.

"*Trydd.*" Vivienne's magic was added.

"*Oleanff.*" And finally, Martin completed the circle.

The room erupted into blue radiance, visions of stars, and the smell of roses as we drifted into the netherworlds. I whispered, "Joyeuse Garde," and let my tracking spell do its work.

Illuminated colours bounced off the weightless ether around us, encompassing everything in a prism of hues and light. We floated along, searching for signs of Joyeuse Garde, until a pocket dimension materialized at the edge of a dark corner of the netherspace. I reached out gently—spinning a magical thread—and sensed the faint essence of Morgawse and Nostradamus. I took a breath and drew our combined magic into myself.

I chanted, "*Mwn lau a syr, mwn dwyr a thyll, gwis ger rhwymdd o gwmas y bydd hwyn. Ewh atgwy, cloyn dynnth. Gedwch i ynrhyw benth adayl eille.*"

Between the void and earth, between the darkness and the light, through the weft of reality and the impossible, I entwined our infused energy, twisting our magic around Joyeuse Garde in a fabric of binding. It strengthened and grew at my command, morphing into a wall of glowing thorns constricting the pocket space and sealing it shut. When the last bit of magic tucked itself into place, Michel screamed in rage.

I whispered, "It's done." Then I closed my eyes and returned us all to the office. I calmed my breath to steady myself and opened my eyes. Four pale shaking figures stared back at me.

"That will hold them for a while, but Nostradamus and Morgawse will find a way to break the spell eventually. We need some preparation, but we'll leave for Tintagel in," I glanced at the clock on the wall, "a half hour."

I turned to Vivienne. "Is the Tintagel portal still active at the lake?"

She nodded.

"Good. To the kitchen, then. I think there are some scones left, and there's ham for sandwiches. Some midnight fortification is in order before we leave."

"Sounds good." Morgan moved past me, followed by Iseult who said, "I'll make tea."

The rest of us followed.

AFTER FILLING our bellies on ham sandwiches, scones and tea we now stood at the edge of Vivienne's lake under the stars. I clenched my jaw, thinking of happy things to keep myself from conking the bunch of whiners surrounding me.

I stared at Vivienne's back as she went into a trance to activate the portal. To my right, Morgan complained about her ugly boots and the insects, to my left, Iseult cursed Mark repeatedly in at least three languages and Martin kept asking if he had to come along. Thankfully Vivienne got the portal opened before I batted any of them or shoved them into the lake.

I made Morgan go first to prevent any runners, then Iseult and Martin, with Vivienne and I bringing up the rear, and we landed safely beside the well ruins on the southern cliffs. The other end of the portal was magically camouflaged but at that time of night, the place was empty of people.

I marched forward waving the others along with my electric torch, and barking, "Come on, it's this way."

I led the others past the chapel to some dark age

ruins, the lot of us huffing and puffing as we hiked the rough, hilly terrain in the dark.

"How did you find out about Mark's hideaway?" Morgan asked.

I glanced at her, wondering whether she inquired to make conversation or mischief. With a grin, I replied, "I keep an eye on things. I have spies everywhere."

She glared at me and stopped asking nosy questions.

We arrived at the rather nondescript spot and the rest milled around while I shone my light on the ground to find the exact spot. It took a minute, and I then dusted some leaves and dirt off the symbol that activated the portal. Next I dug some portal dust out of my bag, sprinkled it over the stone and straightened.

"Gather in close. No stragglers."

I waited until everyone moved nearer and then spoke the spell word to trigger the entrance to Mark's private netherworld.

"*Yngyre.*"

In a sparkle of light, the ruins of Tintagel melted away and all five of us stood on a paved path lined by rose bushes and rows of lilies under a blue sky and sunshine. A short distance away loomed a tall, fairytale-like castle.

I grunted. "Welcome to Mark's abode. Lovely and pretentious, isn't it?" Behind me, Iseult whimpered. I sighed. "Let's get this over with."

I stepped forward, my boots thumping on the stone walkway, the heady floral scent of the plant life ushering me along. The footsteps of the others trailed in my wake and we followed the path until we stood in front of the imposing arched door to the castle.

Behind me, Morgan quipped, "What, no moat? No drawbridge?"

For a moment I grinned. In my best haughty American, I replied, "Those are *so* passé." Then I grabbed the dragon-shaped door knocker and announced our arrival in a series of loud beats.

The booming noise and echo undercut the silence of the place and jolted our fraying nerves. Morgan jumped at the sound, Martin whimpered, and Vivienne shrieked. I glanced over at Iseult. She looked as though she might vomit at any moment.

We stood there for several minutes, staring at the wooden barrier of a door. Thoughts banged in my head against memories and I wanted nothing more than to turn tail and run. I gritted my teeth on an inhale of breath and tried to release my doubts and fears with the exhale. Finally, footsteps sounded within the castle structure.

We waited, with whimpers and bated breath, until the massive door creaked slowly open and we stood face-to-face with…

A griffin.

"Greetings. Welcome to Castle Dore. Please enter. My master has been waiting for you." The griffin stepped aside and waved a wing in a sweeping gesture to usher us within the castle.

I blinked. Not only a griffin, a talking griffin with the mannerisms and accent of a proper English butler. I shrugged and walked inside, followed by the others. The griffin moved ahead of us, its front talons clacking on the marble floor.

"If you will accompany me, I shall take you to Master Mark. He has been most anxious to see you all." The creature glanced back at Iseult. "Especially you, ma'am.

He is most desirous to make amends."

She growled, "The feeling is not mutual. I'm here under duress."

The griffin nodded in a sympathetic manner. "I can imagine. As I understand it, my master has been most unpleasant in his dealings with you. However, he is a changed man. You will see." The beast fluttered a wingtip. "He is not seeking absolution, merely asking to offer apologies. You are free to accept or reject at your own discretion."

Iseult's expression changed to slight shock and inside I echoed her mood. The whole surreal traipse down the hallways felt unnerving and blanketed in tense silence.

"Here we are, my master's study." The griffin sat on his haunches, reached up a front talon and turned the doorknob. "Go in; he's waiting for you." Then the creature walked off, leaving us staring at the partially open doorway. I pushed it wider and we all reluctantly strolled into the room.

Mark sat behind an enormous mahogany desk, wearing a velvet smoking jacket and holding a pipe. Of all the scenarios, this was not what I had expected. Iseult snorted and Morgan laughed. I glanced behind me and Vivienne had already made herself comfortable in a chair and Martin was trying to hide behind his grandmother. Mark flashed a smile and then rose to his feet.

He walked around the desk and greeted us. "Welcome, I'm glad you decided to come. I feared you would not." He held his hand out to me and I shook it.

"I didn't really have much of a choice. None of us did."

Mark nodded solemnly. "Yes, choices are limited in this matter."

I noticed he avoided looking at Iseult. She, on the other hand, glared at him with a fierce, intense hatred. He ignored her animosity and instead focused on Martin, walking over to him. Mark held out his hand and Martin shook it gingerly, looking at his grandmother while he did so.

"You must be Iseult's grandson. It is a pleasure to meet you. I hope you enjoyed my gift."

That sent Iseult off. "Your gift? You mean my spellbook, the one you stole from me? And then gave to him as *your* gift. How dare you interfere like that? Bringing him into magic as you did. I could kill you for that alone, if you could actually die."

"Ah, I can see how you might have interpreted it as interference, but I was only following the Lady's instructions. All will become clear when I explain."

I snorted. "So this Lady told you to steal Iseult's spellbook, send it to Martin, and turn him into a wizard?" I put my hands on my hips and gave him my best disbelieving look.

"No, she told me to make Martin a wizard. The method was mine. It seems young Martin has his own destiny to fulfil." Mark tugged at his shirt cuffs, but didn't elaborate. He only added, "I was also supposed to bring the two of you together but Elaine was kind enough to make that happen without my help."

I glared. "And of course, it didn't hurt that Iseult might get involved once Martin had the spellbook. Right?"

He nodded. "The Lady wanted Iseult involved as well. The spellbook seemed the most expedient way to link you all and send the message."

"What, you don't have a phone in this place?" Morgan chimed in with her two cents. "All these stratagems seem excessive, but you always were one for fancy games and convoluted goings-on."

Mark smirked. "Actually, I don't have a phone in the castle. You can't get any good mobile reception and the landline bill would be outrageous."

I nearly chuckled at the dumbfounded expression on Morgan's face.

Mark sniffed before continuing, "Enough of this pleasant chit-chat. You've come on business, on a quest to seek Merlin's grimoire." He leaned against the mahogany desk.

"We have." I scowled. "We also have a mad wizard and Morgawse on our tail. As you well know since you sent us on this quest. Let's get this over and done."

"I did begin this," Mark shrugged, "or rather it was the Lady. And I have what you seek, or at least the key to it. The rest will be up to you. But first I need to speak with Iseult. Nimue, you may stay, but the rest of you, if you could give us some privacy. Wander the castle, do a little exploring. You won't get lost; all the corridors and passages lead back to the front hall."

Iseult stood there with her arms crossed and stamped her foot but didn't say a word. I studied the back wall, while the others shuffled out of the room, closing the door behind them.

I dropped down into a chair. "Say your piece, Mark. I don't think she's going to give you another shot."

I watched Mark stare at Iseult and wondered what was going on in his head. The anger radiated off her like a sun, and her entire posture screamed 'I don't want to be here' and 'I hate you'.

He took a step forward. "I'm sorry." The words came out gently, almost as a whisper. "I behaved badly towards you and was a terrible husband, if you could even call me a husband. I was controlling, jealous and treated you more like property than a person. For all of that, I am sorry. For all the harassment, the stalking, and the misery I put you through, I am truly regretful." He sighed, the sound carrying a thousand lifetimes of contrition and the lament of what might have been.

"I can never undo what I did or atone for my mistakes. I can only offer you my sincere apologies and my promise that it is over. I will never bother you again and, if you wish it, this is the last time you ever have to see me. I hope that one day you can forgive me but I do not ask it, nor expect it. We can part here forever and you will be free of me and my attention."

Mark then stepped back and walked around his desk. He stooped and opened a drawer, retrieving a small box from inside. Iseult stood still, watching Mark move, saying nothing. The look on her face was cold and blank, and her body remained stiff and rigid, her fingers clenched into fists. As Mark straightened, he looked at me not her. Then he held out the box.

"This is what you'll need to find the grimoire. Inside is the key that will unlock a portal to Annwn and show you the way to the grimoire's hiding place in Caer Wydyr. Take it to Arthur's tomb. There's a glyph on the wall behind the casket, in the shape of a hound and stag. In the middle of this glyph will be a keyhole. Use the key to reveal the portal."

I nodded, took the box and tucked it in my satchel.

"That's it?" Iseult's irritated voice broke through. "An apology and a key? That's all you're going to say? You're not going to try and talk me into staying, into being your wife again? You're not going to hold me here against my will or some other stupidity that you've tried in the past?"

Mark looked at her. "No. You're free to go and never return. You will never hear from me again."

"I—I don't—" Iseult stammered, her face a muddled expression of anger, shock and confusion. She turned and stalked out of the room.

"I hope you meant what you said, Mark, and you'll leave her alone." I rose and extended my hand in goodbye. "I don't understand what's going on with you, but hope you have changed and can find some happiness."

He grasped my hand and squeezed it briefly. "Thank you. I have found peace, at least. Perhaps happiness will come in time." He dropped my hand and took a step back. "You should go and find the others. Time is of the essence and you should begin as soon as possible."

I nodded, but was determined to not leave without answers. "About this Lady of yours. Who is she and what does she want with me? Her name wouldn't happen to be Gwenevere, would it?"

He shook his head. "Gwenevere serves the Lady. As I do. As we all do in our own way."

I glared. "That's not an answer. Who is she? All this subterfuge and pussy-footing around is pissing me off."

Mark chuckled. "For you, I have no doubt her methods seem irritating, but she is who she will be. And you'll find out your answers in time."

"Of all the—"

An enormous crack of thunder broke the air and the walls of the castle shook. A roaring voice boomed, the words echoing around the room. "In the name of Nostradamus, send out the book! Or we will tear this place to the ground and take it!"

"What the bloody hell?" I raced out the study, running towards the front entrance, Mark at my heels. Morgan and Vivienne sprinted down another hallway, heading for us. Mark and I rushed outside, followed by the other two women.

Above us, on wings of black and gold, flew a horde of dragons.

Instinctively, I whispered, "*Anwybyd*" and blasted a wave of flames at the beasts. The formation split in two, flanking the battlements and raining down fire of their own on the castle and the surrounding area.

"Damnation and bloody hell!" I dove for cover behind some singed roses and shook my fist at the sky. I scanned the area. Vivienne and Morgan had retreated back inside the castle doorway. Mark crouched beside the next bush down.

"Tell me you have defenses in this place."

"Of course." Mark laughed and then shouted, "*Ffrwyd amddiffyn fatan gwyllyt!*"

The sky exploded with a barrage of fireworks and the dragons roared. The air echoed with the furious beating of their wings as the assault of pyrotechnics rained down on them.

Then he barked at me, "Gather your friends and find Gerald. He'll take you to the tunnels and get you out. Let me handle these intruders." He tossed a few fireballs into the sky before adding, "Remember the dragon crest!"

I hesitated and then ran for the castle.

Then Mark shouted, "*Eyth mi Gryffyns!*"

I looked back and suddenly the sky was crowded with hundreds of griffins, swooping down to attack the dragons, slashing at them with their talons and shredding the edges of their wings with their beaks. Mark stood on the path, arms raised to the sky, laughing like a maniac; magic energy lanced from his fingertips at his enemies.

Then I dashed through the door, dragging Morgan and Vivienne with me, racing on into the interior of the castle. Halfway down the corridor leading past Mark's study, we saw Iseult and Martin running towards us from yet another passageway and Gerald half-flying, half-loping down behind them.

I didn't leave them anytime to ask questions, shouting, "Nostradamus sent dragons to attack the castle! Mark's fighting them off with griffins. He wants us to escape through the tunnels." Even as I said it, I knew how peculiar it all sounded and ignored the shocked stares and exclamations of "What?" from Martin and Iseult and the snorting laughter from Morgan.

Gerald, on the other hand, took it much better, barking, "Follow me, the tunnels are this way." He raced off down a hall to the left and we chased after him.

We madly dashed through the castle—the walls

reverberating with the thunderous roar of the beasts outside—until we reached an iron door. Gerald yanked it open and we fled down rickety stairs. Candles magically ignited on the walls, their flickering flames showing ancient wooden steps and dirty stone walls dripping with damp and moss.

We descended into this derelict underground, our footsteps pounding on the wood, the stench of moulding earth and forgotten time wafting up. At the bottom of the stairs, several tunnels branched out and we followed Gerald into one to our right.

We sprinted down the long tunnel in gasping breath, legs aching, until we finally arrived at the end. Gerald turned, his wings drawn tight to his body, his beak clacking softly. "Go on without me. The portal is active and just beyond here in the courtyard. Speak the name of where you wish to be and walk through. I must return to my master."

Somehow he slipped by all of us and raced back the way we came.

"Shit." I cursed under my breath, but we kept moving until we emerged in a courtyard. A foot ahead of us stood a glowing portal archway. "There's the way out of here." Hope and relief blossomed.

"Where will we go?" Martin's voice trembled.

"Arthur's tomb," I replied and ran through the portal.

Chapter Thirteen

To Annwn

We shuffled around King Arthur's final resting place, all of us at a loss.

I kept glancing at the carved sarcophagus, memories stirring. Visions of Merlin, Camelot, that day I helped him weave the stasis spell, and when we placed Arthur into his eternal slumber. I never understood the reasons behind any of it.

I walked over and placed a hand on the casket. "I remember when we laid him to rest."

My voice echoed slightly. I stroked the symbols along the edge and felt the magic tingle under my touch. I glanced behind me at the sound of footsteps. Morgan moved beside me, gently brushing her fingertips against the wood.

"It was raining. When we brought him here." Deep sadness resonated in her voice.

I patted her hand. Sometimes I forgot Arthur was her half-brother. "I'm sorry. This must be difficult."

"Visiting him always is, no matter what the reason." She traced part of a bear symbol that ran most of the length of the coffin. "But it was what he wanted. His choice. I had to respect that. We all did in the end." She withdrew her hand. "But that's not why we're here today. Best stop all this reminiscing and get on with it."

I nodded. "Look for a symbol on the back wall; a hound and stag. That's what we need to find."

She turned and walked towards the wall behind the casket.

I remained standing at Arthur's entombed body. I closed my eyes and reached out; I couldn't help myself. I sensed his heartbeat from inside the stasis, a quiet rhythmic thump of life.

Memories raced through my mind.

Merlin was angry that day. He hit me for asking why

we needed the safeguards, why we needed to lock the stasis spell to our specific magicks. I never understood why he granted only the two of us the ability to wake Arthur. Merlin said it was to protect him, but it seemed like a lie. Although, if I had done that with Morgawse we might not be in this mess.

Arthur was drunk when we came for him. He babbled on about Mordred, betrayal, and how destiny had cost him everything. His last words before the spell took effect were, "It isn't fair." He had that right. None of it was fair.

But still, how could Arthur choose that? Sleeping for eternity. It seemed so unlike the man I knew. But after what Mordred did… well, maybe even immortals can't live with a broken heart.

I let out a breath, drifting from the past and opened my eyes. I walked around the coffin to join the others, who were all standing in front of the glyph Mark had told us to find.

Etched deep into the stone and painted white, it was a traditional Celtic symbol, a simple hound chasing a stag. I leaned in, trying to see the keyhole that Mark had mentioned but nothing resembled an opening. I moved my fingers over the stone, tracing the engraving and suddenly the figures shifted.

The symbols contorted to reshape themselves; each figure now stood on their hind legs. The hound and stag faced each other and in the center appeared a small keyhole. I reached into my satchel, withdrew the key Mark had given me, and inserted it. I twisted until the lock clicked.

Every glyph, symbol, and rune on the wall Illuminated in a glowing blue light and the radiance flowed like water, interconnecting and spreading. The entire surface transformed from stone to magical light and within moments became a shimmering portal.

I inhaled deeply and slowly exhaled. "On the other side of this portal is Annwn. This isn't a welcoming place. Stay together and don't wander off. We want to get in and out as quickly as possible."

Everyone nodded.

"Here we go then." I took another deep breath and stepped through the portal.

I emerged in a field of blue and golden flowers, the breeze carrying the scent of cowslip and bluebells. Overhead an indigo sky twinkled in stars and moonlight, shining a bright luminescence over everything. I moved forward, drinking in the sheer wonder of it all, only turning back at the exclamations of the others as they arrived.

As Vivienne, the last through the portal, entered Annwn, a small thread of magic snaked past her and spun across the air. It wove out from the closing portal like a loose strand of yarn and darted forward into the distance beckoning us onward.

"We follow the magic thread, I guess." I started off, chasing Mark's magical guide.

Morgan muttered, "What, no breadcrumbs?" but everyone fell in line and we commenced our journey.

"Be careful and don't stray off the path," I admonished as Martin gawked at his surroundings. "This place can be dangerous. And avoid the swallows at all costs. They'll peck your eyes out." Martin gulped and scurried closer to Vivienne.

The strand of light led us through the field and then veered off to a stony path. We tramped along that trail for some time, before changing course again into a field of primroses. The starlight twinkled off the pink and yellow flowers and a sweet fruity fragrance wafted as we walked. We could have been strolling through an English meadow and I relaxed, letting my tension flow away with the breeze.

Until we heard the growling.

Shit.

We all came to a dead stop. Martin whimpered. Morgan raised her fists like a boxer. Iseult and Vivienne stepped closer, glancing over their shoulders. I scanned the field, trying to see over the rise ahead, looking for shadows as a soft grey mist formed around us. I knew that growl meant trouble.

The Cwn Annwn were near.

Something moved to the right, a shape in the thickening mist. "Maybe we should retreat," I whispered. "A tactical—"

In a flash of red radiance and black sparks, a pack of spectral hounds appeared over the rise, racing towards us in an attack. They lunged at us, jaws slavering, teeth snapping and we scattered in a panic. As I ran, I counted at least half a dozen, maybe more; the fog made it hard to see. Sable flares of energy crackled off their white fur and from their eyes, and their red ears had turned a deep maroon.

Shit! They've been infected with dark magic.

I zigzagged to avoid being hauled down by two hounds and managed to calm down enough to spit out, "*Anwybyth*," and toss off a few fireballs at the beasts. I singed their hides and they fled in a flurry of yelps and howls. Unfortunately I also set the primroses on fire. I fled the flames, straight into the middle of a free-for-all with three hounds, Morgan and Martin.

Morgan wrestled with one hound and was holding her own. Another beast dragged Martin to the ground, teeth tearing his arm. With a wild yell, I waded in to rescue him, but the third hound attacked, going straight for his throat. The hound's teeth ripped open a hole in Martin's neck and his blood sprayed over flowers, fur, and me.

"Bloody fucking hell!" I rushed at both hounds, a thousand points of white-hot fury building inside me. I slammed energy balls into the hounds, knocking them back and senseless. I stood over Martin's body taking in a breath, drawing power from the earth beneath my feet and praying I had enough time to build the force I needed. I barely managed before the hounds recovered, scrabbled back to their feet and attacked again.

My next words shot out with the shriek worthy of a banshee, "*Byed yth byn atmyn eich cyr yff gaelchi eith chwyth uidd arnau!*"

Both creatures glowed red-hot and howled, before exploding in a burst of blood, bone, flesh and fur. Seconds later a dozen more howls and explosions of hounds. I stood there, staring down at Martin's body, dripping in hound guts and gore. The explosions had burnt off the mist and everything was covered in viscera.

"What the hell did you do?" Morgan shook me and spat out a mouthful of blood. She let go when she saw Martin. "Oh. They killed him."

"I used Vold's Spontaneous Combustion Spell." Then Iseult shrieked and anything else I might have said was drowned in her reaction.

She whirled on me. "How did you let this happen? Getting him killed!" Then she punched me in the jaw. I stumbled to my knees, but before I could react or hit back, Morgan hauled her off me. I stood and took a few steps backward.

"Stop with the bloody hysterics, Iseult!" Morgan pinned back her arms as she struggled. "It's not fucking permanent. Not the best way to go for a first death, but he'll revive."

As Iseult settled down, glowering at Morgan, I glanced over at Martin. Vivienne sat on the blood stained grass, holding his head in her lap and stroking his hair. She looked at me. "Poor lamb. A messy death."

I nodded, and looked away. I noticed we were all covered in hound remains.

Messy for all of us.

I inhaled and spat out another spell, "*Chych an rhychwant dyna'rth cynllu.*" Magical energy sparked around each of us, cleaning off gore, guts and washing out the blood stains.

Morgan frowned at me. I shrugged.

"Might as well be comfortable while we wait for Martin to revive."

It took about half an hour for his throat to regenerate and his mangled arm to close up its wounds, helped along by the power of Annwn. Fifteen minutes later his eyelids fluttered open.

He sat up screaming. "Get away! Get away! Get off me!"

"Martin!" My shout cut him off mid-panic. "You're safe now. The hounds are gone. You're fine. You're safe."

"But—But I wasn't safe, was I? They—they *killed* me." He gulped and shivered, crossing his arms and rocking. "They *killed* me."

Vivienne put a hand on his shoulder and crooned, "It's all right; it's all right. The first time's always the hardest. And the longest."

I bit my lip and stuffed away the urge to punch something. I rubbed my jaw. Nothing I could say would make it better. You either accepted immortality or it drove you mad. I turned away when Martin started crying.

I waited until Martin finished processing, and Vivienne and Iseult had helped him to his feet. His face was pale, but he held it together.

"We have to keep moving," I said brusquely and looked for the thread. It hovered a few away, still beckoning. I marched forward, not caring if anyone followed me. Yet, they did.

SEVERAL COMPLAINTS and whines—plus moans of sore feet, bruises, and aching muscles—later, we arrived at the foot of Caer Wydyr. There the thread stopped, falling loosely to the ground. I stared at the towering hill, while everyone else flopped on the ground to rest.

The Caer—an enormous stone fortress—perched on a massive hillside that dominated the surrounding landscape and loomed like a protective shadow. Crenellated walls and round towers spread out over the hilltop, all surrounding interior buildings. To the right, a path and a stone stairway wound up the hill to the Caer. As I studied the thing, a knot grew in my stomach.

Behind me came the soft pad of footsteps, and Vivienne placed a hand on my shoulder. "It looks different from the last time we were here. Then it was smaller, softer, more like a hill fort. Now it seems more like an English castle from the Middle Ages."

"It changes with the times, you know that, and with the whims of the creatures that live here." I bit my lip. "That's why I hate coming here. It's so unpredictable. Not to mention dangerous." I shook off Vivienne's hand. "I suppose we'd better climb and see if we can get inside."

As I spoke, the thread shimmered into life again. A piece broke off and flew at me, hovering in front of my face. I defensively raised my arm and it circled my limb. Curious, I extended my hand, and the glowing thread settled into my palm, transforming into a key.

"Well, isn't that a fun parlour trick?" I closed my fingers over the key and held it up for the others to see. "Apparently we have a way in. At least I'm assuming that's what it is." I tucked the key into my satchel. "Come on, let's get started. It's going to be a long climb." I headed out along the path, followed by groans and then shuffling footsteps.

As we ascended the stone stairs for the long climb, the sky above us darkened, the starlight dimmed, and the moon shifted behind strange grey clouds. The wind blew with fierce intensity, a chill to its breath nipping at our skin, and the skies opened into a downpour.

I turned up the collar of my jacket against the heavy rain, listening to the moans and groans of the others. By the time we reached the top, we were thoroughly soaked, miserable and cranky. And then, of course, the rain stopped.

I ground my teeth, muttering, "I hate netherworlds," and angrily stomped through a puddle towards the gatehouse and a large wooden door in the wall. As I got close enough for a good look, I stopped. The door was smooth, not a handle, not an iron ring, not a keyhole. No way to open it at all.

"Bloody hell, I'm getting sick and tired of all these entrances with no way to enter. Can't these damn places ever have just an ordinary door with a bloody keyhole ready to put the key in?"

Then my satchel started shaking and banging. I opened the flap and the key flew out, spinning in the air and gliding to the door. It hovered for a moment, shimmering until a matching glow appeared in the middle of the door and a keyhole materialized. Then the key agreeably turned itself in the lock and the door opened on its own.

"Seems we have an invitation."

So we entered the Caer and the door slammed shut behind us. This time, the key remained on the outside of the door. We walked across the ward and torches along the walls burst into flame. Martin jumped and then gave a low exclamation of delight. Ahead of us, I saw the main keep. Another door creaked open, and we moved inside.

The walls and the floor shone in a sparkling white marble and inlaid mother-of-pearl. Flaming candles blazed along the walls, flickering light and shadows along the myriad halls that branched out, beckoning us further into the interior of the fortress.

Martin moved beside me, his expression afraid. "Will we find more monsters? What lives here? This place looks like a home for monsters."

I put a hand on his shoulder, and answered, "Monsters used to live here, but not wicked ones. They're gone now, and the Caer is empty. It's only a sad memorial to other times when magic had more power."

My answer seemed to satisfy him and the tension relaxed in his shoulders. Vivienne quietly moved to his other side and gave him a hug. Her presence seemed to reassure him.

I frowned. *What's that all about? When did they get chummy?*

I pulled my attention away, and stepped forward to study the maze of hallways spreading out in front of us. I noticed each corridor had an arched doorway with an etched symbol above it, in the form of a heraldic animal. I frowned, something tickling at the back of my thoughts, and Mark's last words to me flashed in my head.

I glanced back at the others. "Above the doors, see the symbols? Look for a dragon crest. I'd wager that's where we need to go."

Morgan grinned at me. "I get it. Merlin's sigil. You think Mark left a signpost on the correct doorway?"

I nodded, and the next few minutes were spent scanning the walls until Iseult shouted, "I found it! Over here."

She stood to the far left, in front of a carved wooden archway, painted blue. We rushed over, and sure enough, chiselled in the stone wall above the arch, was a dragon carving.

A shiver ran across my skin and the magic in my blood prickled. "That's it. That's the way we need to go."

With no hesitation I marched down the corridor, the others scrambling after me.

We trudged a twisting circular route that, I swear, doubled back on itself at least twice. We finally exited into a large library that looked as if it had been plucked out of a Victorian gothic novel.

Muted light illuminated the room, but from what source I couldn't say. No lamps or candles hung on the walls or sat on the furniture. Hundreds of dark wooden shelves lined the walls and held thousands of leather-bound books. I gaped at the treasure trove of knowledge.

As we moved further inside, I spun around taking in the wonder of the library. Most of the volumes waited for a reader to pluck them from the open shelving, but others beckoned from behind glass cases next to knickknacks and other peculiar objects. A few rectangular tables and high-backed chairs were scattered across the room and a grand stairway wound upward to a balcony. I presumed it led to another level of the strange chamber. I smiled at the beauty of it all.

Beside me, Martin gave a small exclamation of glee.

"Look at all the books!" His face blossomed in joy and I remembered he used to run a bookshop.

For a moment I shared his happiness. Then it hit me. "Mark hid the grimoire in a library." I inhaled deeply to calm myself. "We're going to have to bloody search for it."

Groans sounded behind me, but Martin looked positively eager.

He shouted, "Let's get started," and moved forward. I caught him by the elbow and dragged him to a halt.

"Wait a minute. You don't even know what you're looking for."

He turned around with a sheepish grin. "Oh, yeah. Right. So what's this tome look like, then?"

"It's made of vellum, bound in faded blue leather over a wooden cover. There's a figure of a golden dragon running down its spine, with a gold triskelion embossed on the front. There are also several ogham symbols scattered over the cover. At least, that's what it looked like when I last saw it." I glanced at everyone to make sure they understood. "However, if you find it, don't touch it. It can be crotchety about who handles it. Just shout and I'll deal with it."

Vivienne, Iseult and Martin moved off, Martin nearly skipping in glee, and the other two mumbling and whinging under their breath.

Morgan lingered for a moment, asking, "Will you be able to deal with it? It may hold a grudge, considering the bad blood between you and Merlin."

"Maybe, but the book always responded well to me. Sometimes more than Merlin, which ticked the bloody sod off considerably."

Morgan chuckled. "I'm not surprised. Nothing annoyed him more than someone or something ignoring his self-perceived greatness."

I nodded. "Very true." I looked around the room. "Better get to work. This search could take a while." Morgan moved off to the left, while I decided to tackle the upper level.

I climbed the staircase, enjoying the feel of the smooth wood of the banister under my fingertips and admiring the craftsmanship in the construction. I wondered how much of it was real and how much a glamour illusion. In Annwn, it was always hard to tell.

I reached the top and began examining the books for Merlin's grimoire. Below, the others did the same, and we all settled into our hunt.

"OH MY, the entire set of *Le Marchand's Spells and Incantations*." Morgan's ecstatic squeal echoed throughout the room, snapping my attention away from the umpteenth pass of the bookshelves at the back of the upper level.

I cursed and rushed out to the balcony railing, peering over the edge. Morgan pulled three books from a shelf and headed off. I yelled down, "Morgan! Stop getting distracted! We don't have time for side projects!"

She ignored me and plunked the volumes and herself at a table and started reading.

I scowled, knowing I'd lost her, and went back to the search. From below, Martin recited names like a cheerful cartoon chipmunk as he poured over the books and Vivienne hummed to herself, some country tune she enjoyed and I hated. Iseult didn't say much except for the occasional muttered complaint but her footsteps stalked through the room to the right.

I checked my watch. If it was accurate, we'd only been there twenty minutes.

Shit. It's going to be a long day.

I moved past the balcony and started examining another shelf further along the upper level.

An hour later, I leaned against a wall staring at rows of books wondering if I should invoke a fire spell and just burn the place down. Luckily for the library, Iseult shouted and grabbed everyone's, including Morgan's, attention.

"I found something. Not the book, but I think there's another room."

I trotted down the stairs with renewed hope, or at least less bored. The others were already lined up in a far corner, clustered around a life-size painting of the Morrigan. I repressed a shiver and tried not to stare at the representation of the black-clad figure on a blood-soaked battlefield, surrounded by ravens.

I turned to Iseult instead. "What did you find?"

"That this painting," she grabbed the frame of the monstrous artwork, "is hinged." She pulled on the frame and it swung outward, revealing a door. "Hiding the entrance to another room." She reached over, turned the handle and pushed the door inward.

We crowded inside and then stopped in our tracks.

Cold white grins greeted us from the long-dead skulls of three skeletons. All three corpses were dressed in the ragged remains of medieval-style clothing and tarnished chain mail, with rusted weapons belted about their waists. One body sprawled on the floor at a twisted angle, its vacant eye sockets staring up at us, while the other two were seated in chairs as if waiting for their tea.

Martin screeched, as did his grandmother, both sounds remarkably similar. I noted the fascinating family resemblance but was more interested in the platform beyond the bodies. A book bound in blue leather with a gold triskelion on the cover rested on top of the stand.

"There it is. Finally. Merlin's grimoire."

At the sound of its name, the stand shook and the floor trembled slightly. The skeletons' bones rattled, and as one, all three dead men rose on bony limbs. Facing us, their bare white fingers clacked as they placed decayed hands upon tarnished swords.

I whispered softly, "Vivienne, Iseult, take Martin and back out of the room slowly." Their feet shuffled and the skeleton guards shifted their stance, although they did not move forward. I added, "Very slowly."

The three of them backed out of the room as quiet as lost ghosts. The dead did not advance.

"Morgan," as I said her name, all three skeletons turned to look at her. I repressed a shudder at their creepy unison of movement. "Be prepared, but don't move unless they attack. If they do, then magically kick the shit out of them."

From the corner of my eye, she nodded slightly and murmured an indistinct, "Mmmhmm."

I took a deep breath and then exhaled, stepping one foot forward. The skeletons' gaze snapped back to me with the cracking and creaking of bone. I took another step. Their boney fingers tightened over sword hilts. One more step and they clacked their jaws, teeth clattering in an ear-splitting racket. Their skulls tilted backward and deep mournful howls somehow emanated from their hollow throats.

Their heads snapped forward again with open jaws, and as one disembodied voice they spoke. "Play the game. Tell your name. If it's true, we let you through."

I scowled, silently cursing all riddles and rhymes. But I replied, "Nimue."

As one they moved apart, creating a path to the grimoire. "You have been expected. You may pass. But only you." Their skulls whipped about to stare at Morgan briefly and then back at me. "The book is yours if it will have you."

I moved gingerly past the dead, barely breathing until I was next to the grimoire. I shifted sideways to keep my eye on the skeleton guard, not quite trusting them, and placed the fingertips of my right hand on the grimoire.

I leaned in and whispered, "*Banba.*"

A soft hum drifted out from the pages along with a golden glow. Tiny sparks crackled from the triskelion emblem and threads of magic twisted around my fingers. My hand shaking, I lifted the grimoire from the stand. I clasped it to my chest, crossing my arms around it, and turned to leave.

All three guardians blocked my way, their hollowed-out eye sockets staring at me from their grinning skulls.

Behind them, a glow crept around Morgan's fingers and I felt a faint hint of her magic. I took a breath, preparing for a fight, until one of the corpses turned his skull around with a loud crack of his neck, so what remained of his face stared directly at Morgan.

He said, "We are not your enemy. Don't change that."

I watched the glow fade from Morgan's hand and waited.

The other two dead men spoke together, addressing me, "The book is yours, yet we remain. Our bones will rot and our spirits are yours to summon."

As the echo of the incorporeal words faded, all three skeletons collapsed onto the floor, bones turning to dust under piles of rotting cloth and broken weapons. I skirted around the disintegrated guardians, grabbed a dumbfounded Morgan and dashed out the door of the secret chamber. I turned back to look, but the door slammed shut and the painting swung back into place. I stared for a moment, and I swore the figure of the Morrigan grinned at me. Then I turned away, to see the anxious faces of Iseult, Vivienne, and Martin.

Vivienne clapped her hands. "You got the grimoire!"

I looked down, suddenly aware I was still holding the book. "I did." I glanced over at the painting, unsettled.

Morgan flopped down in a nearby chair. "What the hell happened in there? What was that last bit of shit?"

I shrugged. "I don't know." Morgan gave me a skeptical stare. "Really. No clue, but it doesn't bode well."

Martin abruptly broke the tension, asking, "How do we get out of here then? Our way in deserted us back at the entrance to this place."

"That's easy. This place has a built-in exit portal." I walked over to a table and placed the grimoire gently on the surface. "Merlin's book has a spell to activate it."

"Oh, I remember that," Vivienne chimed in, as the others stared at her. She didn't elaborate.

I flipped through the grimoire's pages, the familiar feel and magic reassuring my soul and soothing my nerves, until I found the right spell.

"Here we are. This will activate the portal and take us right back to the cottage."

I re-familiarized myself with the spell and memorized

the words, closing the book. I picked it up and walked to a spot clear of furniture.

"Gather in behind me. The portal is built into every room, so I can activate it from here and go home." As everyone settled into place, I cleared my throat. "*Rawyr ar gwynth, olwch athaear, yrwyf yn galwyr fford Dadref.*"

From the library floor rose a great glowing archway, a shimmering and shining thing of green light. Beyond it, I could hear birds and smell the sweet scent of roses.

"There it is. The way home." We moved forward together and stepped through.

Chapter Fourteen

Confrontations

Almost immediately something went wrong. The light around us changed from green to grey and the exiting side of the portal snapped shut, tossing us head over arse tumbling into a void. We descended into blackness, screaming, falling between netherworlds.

I hugged the grimoire while frantically trying to pull my satchel forward and being bounced against the others. I managed to get a hand inside my bag when a sizzling force of energy slammed into everyone. It knocked us sideways while simultaneously opening three separate portals. Iseult and Martin got sucked into one, Vivienne another, with Morgan and I yanked into the third.

We were thrown out into a grassy field, rolling to a stop by an old wooden fence. I pushed myself up off the grass spitting out dirt and vegetation and staring at a sunrise. Then I realized I wasn't holding the grimoire anymore. I glanced up and saw the familiar blue leather laying at the feet of Nostradamus. Morgawse stood behind him, scowling at us.

Beside me, Morgan softly growled and scrambled to her feet, magic already dancing off her fingertips. I rose slowly, muscles aching, as I watched Nostradamus pick up the grimoire.

"An excellent try, Nimue, locking us away, but you lose. I will save magic from its own destruction. You will not be allowed to let it die. I have all I need in here." He patted the book and I noticed red sparks snap off the binding.

"I don't think she likes you. Working the spell might not be as easy as you think." I moved a step closer. "And you're wrong about me. I'm the new saviour of magic, or didn't you get the memo?" I savoured the shock on his face. I chuckled as he bristled in anger. Morgawse turned her head towards him, stifling a laugh.

Nostradamus gave me a look of disdain. "What are

you blathering about?"

"What, can't imagine the hero won't be you?" I sniffed and shrugged. "Well, you see, Vivienne..." To my left, Morgan moved forward. I shot a look at Morgawse, adding, "You remember Viv, don't you, Morgawse?" The witch turned her attention to me, as I wanted. "Viv's our seer, isn't she, Morgawse? And she saw how you got it all wrong. You can't save magic."

Nostradamus gasped, but Morgawse's reaction surprised me. She looked happy.

Then an energy ball hit her smack in the chest and she went flying. Nostradamus yelped and I zapped the prat with a jolt of my own magic. The book flew out of his hands and dropped onto the grass.

I raced to grab it, but he recovered faster than I'd anticipated and intercepted me. I punched the bastard in the face and he stumbled back. Then he kicked at the grimoire, connecting a glancing blow, and sent it skidding over the grass. It stopped just behind Morgan and Morgawse who were simultaneously trying to fry each other with magic and claw each other's eyes out.

I hesitated for a moment and Nostradamus quickly formed an energy sphere. I braced for an attack, but his gaze swung towards Morgan. I shouted a warning, but seconds later he blasted her with a bolt of powerful magic.

She went down with a scream, flung well past her sister and slammed back into the earth. She lay still, not a movement or groan. Morgawse stared at her sister, her face pale. Then she turned on Nostradamus and slammed a burst of magic straight into his gut. He tumbled onto his back, moaning. He tried to crawl to his knees but Morgawse hit him again. He stayed down, breathing heavily and squirming in pain.

Morgawse screamed, "She's mine! Hands off!" But she didn't hit him again.

I, on the other hand, had no such scruples. I dashed over and kicked him hard in the ribs. "That's for turning into such an arsehole!" Then I sprinted off, heading to snatch back the grimoire.

Morgawse got there first.

She plucked the book off the ground, holding it like a trophy and laughing. "I can be free with this! I can rule the world with this!"

I skidded to a stop, yelling, "Drop it, bitch!"

Before I could act, it was Morgawse's turn to scream.

Merlin's grimoire sent off a burst of red sparks scorching Morgawse's hands and she flung the book like it was on fire. Which is probably how it felt. I'd been on the receiving end of the book's ire once and my hand had felt seared to the bone.

I watched the book land with a thump on the grass, directly between us. I gleefully laughed, crowing, "The book remembers you, Morgawse. And it holds a grudge, I guess." I moved forward, snatching the grimoire back to safety.

Morgawse shrieked in rage and pain. "That damn magic book! I always hated it!" She pulled her arms into her chest, cradling her hands.

"Give it up, Morgawse. Injured you don't stand a chance. But I'll happily kick your arse if you want." I tucked the book under my arm and conjured up an energy ball, ready to knock her into next Tuesday.

"I'd like to see you try," she snarled.

I readied my attack… until the bloody damn grimoire

slipped from my grasp and conked me on the head. My magic tumbled uselessly away and I stumbled to my knees. The grimoire swooped through the air and a second later Morgawse was down as well. Then the book hovered above all our heads.

Shimmers and sparks exploded off its leather bindings as it opened and a golden glow erupted from the pages. They flipped wildly and then the light engulfed the field. I shielded my eyes with my arm, unable to see anything. The space around me shifted and I was somewhere else.

Chapter Fifteen

Memories of Merlin

I blinked away the lingering flashes of light and golden afterimages. Slowly my vision adjusted and my surroundings came into focus. I sat on a stone bench in an empty chamber facing a stone dais and a book. But not the grimoire. Of that, there was no sign, and no trace of Morgan, Morgawse or Nostradamus.

Only a prison, silence, and that closed book on the dais.

I rose from the bench, walked over to the podium and studied the volume. It appeared ancient but made of paper and leather, not vellum. I traced a finger around the gilt edge of its green leather covering and felt magic radiating off it like a fire in winter.

There was no writing on the cover, nor on the spine; nothing but blank green and gold leather. The book was thick, the paper pages edged with more gold. It smelled slightly musty, slightly of glue and ink. It was the scent of old bookshops and libraries, of my storage trunks and my shelves at home. The aroma of comfort and familiarity.

I opened the cover and my name stared back at me from the first page. Dark green ink inscribed the letters across the parchment, written in old Latin and underneath that, Welsh. As I flipped the page with trembling fingers, my birthdate appeared next, penning itself across the paper as I watched.

I withdrew my hand, not wanting to continue. Familiar anger welled inside me, the deep resentment I carried towards any type of manipulation. I backed away and scowled, and shouted my defiance to the walls.

"Enough with the bloody tricks! I don't know what's going on, but I don't like games!"

Around me the walls suddenly blazed with glowing runes and symbols and the book shook on the dais, its pages flipping forward of their own accord. I backed away a few more steps, a chill against my skin and prickles of distrust and anxiety creeping into my soul.

About halfway through, the book stopped moving and settled to remain open. I stayed rooted to the spot, stubbornly refusing to move. The book rattled on its platform. I stuck out my tongue.

"I said, no games. I'm not playing, whoever is doing this. Go find another patsy."

The book rose in the air and for a second it hovered, before thumping down on the dais hard. Words and letters erupted outward from the pages in a shower of green and black, blue and gold, swirling in the air as if blown on a sharp summer wind. The manifestation of language gusted forward, twirling around me in a whirlwind tornado assault of magic and animated ink.

I felt the magic pierce me to my bones, suck the air out of my lungs and from my surroundings. I fell to my knees, my breath coming in short frantic gasps, consciousness fading away until everything went black.

MY FIRST sensations were of a soft bed, a breeze on my face, and smelling the faint scent of roses. Then I opened my eyes and the sensations disappeared. I stood in a room, looking at myself lying in a Roman-style bed on a straw-stuffed mattress. The shutters were open and a slight wind blew through the hole that served for a window.

I remember this place, this time. I remember lying there and feeling happy.

This was my room in Camelot.

Inwardly I cursed, as it all clicked. The chamber, the book, my name and birthdate. I was in a memory netherworld. Someone, something had cast me into my own memories, back to the one place I never wanted to see again, to the one person…

Footsteps sounded and I turned, knowing who I would see.

Merlin.

I looked back at the *me* in the bed, sick to my stomach and watching the sultry smile on her face as he approached. I wanted to walk over and smack her, to tell her to smarten up and see him for what he was. A user, a manipulator, a louse.

Even if that could happen, I knew it wouldn't work. That girl, that stupid naive version of me, was in love.

I wouldn't have listened if the gods themselves had warned me.

I nearly gagged as Merlin walked over and gave the other me a kiss. I remembered this day, the warm happy feeling I had, the safe little cocoon of lies where I lived still intact. Merlin's next words would change all of that.

I watched him stroke my cheek, his lips parting and his honeyed-tongue spewing his deceptions. "Time to start your lessons today. Time to teach you the secrets of magic."

I couldn't hold it in anymore. I shouted, even knowing none of it was real, it had already happened and I couldn't change any of it. "Don't listen to him! Run. Get up out of that bed, pack your things and run! Go home to your father's inn and live your life. Marry a nice young man, have children, grandchildren, grow old and die. But whatever you do, don't stay here. Don't stay with him! Don't learn magic, don't become a witch." I could feel the tears streaming down my face and heard the trembling in my voice. "Don't become a witch. The price is too high."

I fell silent. I watched her, *me*, laugh and kiss him on the cheek. She whispered in his ear and I knew the words all too well. The joy, the anticipation, the agreement to be his apprentice.

My own private pact with my own private dishonest devil.

"Tell them what they wish to hear, but never what they need to know." I whispered the hard-won truth to the wind. "That's what you said, wasn't it, Merlin, after I found out what magic cost me. And even then I forgave you. Even then I was naive enough to believe you loved me. That immortality wouldn't be so bad, because we would be together. I was such a fool."

I saw myself laugh and fall back on the bed, all my dreams written across my joyful face. That was the last time I was innocent, the last time I had a bright future ahead of me, with no stain on my soul.

I turned away, unable to see who I used to be anymore.

Then the world around me dissolved and I stood inside a dark, dank cave.

I shivered. It felt like the air had dipped several

degrees. I smelled mould and damp decay, and water slithered down the rock walls. In the distance a golden light flickered.

"Magic."

I whispered the word as recognition dawned in my brain. Another memory, another place from my past. The outer tunnel of Merlin's secret cave. His refuge, spelled and hidden, always waiting for him. Where I tucked him away to hibernate for centuries. I wondered if that was why I was here. To relive that day.

Voices drifted out from within his sanctum, drawing me forward. Might as well get this farce over with and play out the memory. I stepped gingerly across the damp cave floor, instinctively trying not to slip, even though this was only an illusion.

I emerged in the magic-carved chamber and my eyes swept the room, gazing at the book-lined shelves chiselled from the rock, his benches holding sheets of inked-scratched vellum, glass bottles and cone-shaped beakers. Stacked earthenware bowls, and his favourite tin and copper chalice were on his spell table. An impossible snapshot from a past best forgotten. All those books rested in my trunks now, the vellum sheets long turned to rot, and the glass only broken shards buried under years. The chalice I had tossed in the Avon River. No doubt it was still there, submerged under centuries of silt.

Standing by one of the benches, my other self and Merlin argued. I didn't have to hear the words to know what they screamed at each other. That last encounter had burned itself into my memory for eternity.

Camelot had fallen months past, and everyone had scattered to the winds. Merlin came to me and showed me a new spell; to put things right, he said. I barely looked at it and refused when he begged me for help. Only as he was leaving did I relent.

I still wonder why I left with him that day.

Did I go because of what had been between us, a vestige of residual love? Or was it grief, wanting to undo the heartbreak, fix something, anything, in that horror of an ending? Or maybe, deep down, I knew Merlin couldn't be allowed to meddle again. That somehow I needed to end his ambitions.

Perhaps I had once known my true motivations,

before guilt, lies, and secrets obscured them over the years. Whatever the reasons, though, the results remained the same.

I watched as the argument escalated, the moment when Merlin pushed me and slammed me against the wall. Then I relived the smack of his fist, knowing it wasn't the first time he had hit me, but it would be the last.

The other me slumped to the floor. In my reality, I barely remembered anything after the blow, but here I was, watching what Merlin did next.

He shuffled through some papers and began preparing his reckless spell, a time spell, the one we had argued over. He muttered to himself, ravings and ramblings, but not working any magic, not yet. He mixed his rare ingredients in one of his glass bottles and then moved back to me, shaking past-me back into consciousness.

I watched myself stare into his face and I remembered the look of madness in his eyes. That same feeling of disgust and horror welled in me as it had that day. A piece of me broke at that moment, transformed by Merlin's fanaticism as surely as if he had cast a spell. I gazed on the fateful second I blasted him with a jolt of magic, slammed him into the table, and then I looked away.

I shouted, "No! I won't watch anymore! I won't relive it!"

I ran from the illusionary chamber and fled back to where I first appeared. Behind me, the room exploded, my magic reacting with his spell ingredients. I stuffed the memories down, covered my ears and closed my eyes.

When I opened them I was standing on a dirt street in front of a timber-framed house with a thatched roof.

I stared. "Where the bloody hell am I?"

Chapter Sixteen

Morgan and Morgawse

I heard footsteps, and a cloaked figure brushed past me. She strode to the door and vigorously knocked. Muffled sounds came from inside, then the door opened halfway. A face peered out at the visitor.

I gasped. Morgawse stood within the interior of the house. She scowled at the cloaked figure.

"What are you doing here?" Morgawse followed her question by spitting in the dirt beside her visitor's feet.

The woman looked down at the spittle, pushing the hood from her face and replied, "Still as genteel as ever, sister?" Morgan glared back at Morgawse. "And why do you think I'm here? Your reckless behaviour. Now, allow me to enter."

Morgawse moved aside with reluctance, opening the door wider, and Morgan walked inside.

Around me, the street scene dissolved and then I stood inside, watching the sisters.

Morgan had shucked her cloak and it lay draped over a wooden chair, one of the few pieces of furniture in the bare room. I frowned at it all, watching the sisters glower at each other in silence, wondering what the bloody hell I was doing there.

This isn't one of my memories. Is it an illusion, a con or...?

"Shit."

The word slipped out and I for a moment I thought I would be caught out. Yet, nothing. I grimaced.

Of course, they didn't hear me. I'm a ghost in someone else's memories. Morgan's or Morgawse's. Maybe both. Another bloody shift in this nonsense of a game.

I shuffled my feet and huffed, "Why the hell was I brought here?"

In answer to my question, green and black words flashed on the wall.

Because you need to observe what transpires. Shut

up and pay attention.

An angry voice pulled my attention away as Morgan snapped at her sister. "How could you! Sacrificing your own son to that dark wizard. I cannot believe you would do such a thing. Even to Mordred."

What? Wait. What was Morgan talking about?

Any irritation towards the snarky magic messenger-on-the-wall evaporated as my full concentration focused on the sisters.

"It's what he wanted." Morgawse turned her head away and for a moment I glimpsed the sorrow on her face. "He wanted to apprentice under the man. Learn more of the dark arts." Her lips narrowed into a hard line and her eyes blinked back tears. "He wanted to be like his mother."

"Did you know what would happen?" Morgan asked her question more gently.

Morgawse whirled, facing her sister, defiant anger in her voice. "No! Never! I would never hurt Mordred. If I had known what that wizard had planned I would have destroyed the bastard first. Instead of after."

Morgan laid a hand on her sister's shoulder.

"Where are they now?"

"I placed what was left of my son in a safe place. Locked in peaceful slumber like Arthur." Morgawse winced. "There's a certain balance in that I think." Then the edge of her mouth curled. "The wizard I sent to a very special netherworld in the care of some rather nasty creatures. He'll suffer an eternity for what he did to my son."

Morgan glanced down for a few minutes before raising her head once more. "That's good. He merited such punishment. Mordred did not deserve that horror." She reached out, and then lowered her arm. "No one need ever know what happened. I've taken care of any trouble that might have arisen from the wizard's disappearance. If the others ever ask of Mordred, I'll tell them I imprisoned him."

"You little liar!" Shock rattled around in my brain as I realized the impact of what Morgan said. All these years I thought Mordred locked away, but something else entirely had happened. Something dark and sinister...

The room shifted underneath me and disappeared.

"Oh fuck it!"

I stumbled as I landed this time, tripping over my

own feet. The smell of violets wafted in the breeze and a beautiful garden surrounded me. Tables and chairs were dotted in among flowers and bushes and waiters brought coffee and pastries to the people seated there. I heard French and the ever annoying beeps and ringtones of modern day technology.

I glanced behind me and saw a brickwork structure and more people; perhaps a hotel or a bed and breakfast. Confused, I wandered further into the garden area. Then I spotted him. Nostradamus. Sitting at a table with a newspaper, a croissant and a café au lait. He sat with a woman, a lovely brunette, slim, poised, who sipped her coffee with dainty precision.

I wanted to strangle her the minute I saw her.

It was Morgan.

Chapter Seventeen

Nostradamus

I stood beside their table, taking turns glaring at each one and shouting my rage to this illusion of a world. Not that they would hear it.

"You knew! You knew he was back and didn't say a word about it! You little conniving, backstabbing bitch! Is that how he found out about Morgawse? Did you tell him? Or maybe you whispered it as some perverted pillow talk. Is that why the two of you are at a hotel? Collusion with a side order of a tryst?"

I took a breath to see Nostradamus put down his newspaper. "Are you ready to tell me yet?" His calm voice spoke in an even tone, but underneath it sliced, edged in menace.

I looked more closely at Morgan and inhaled sharply. Her eyes were glazed over in a shade of grey, dull and lifeless. Her face was pale, her lips devoid of colour. I knew those signs.

I whirled to snarl at Nostradamus even knowing it was a useless gesture. "A marionette spell? What did you do, you bastard, add it to her coffee?"

My words passed through him like the ghost I was, as he interrogated Morgan. "Tell me about what happened to your nephew, Mordred."

"Mordred is gone." Morgan's voice whispered, a monotone of its usual timbre. "He isn't coming home."

"What happened to him? Where is he now?"

"Mordred was betrayed. A dark wizard drained his power and stole his soul, leaving him paralyzed and in a coma. His body is alive, but everything else is gone. Morgawse hid his husk but she never told me where."

Nostradamus leaned forward, the tone of his voice anxious and whining. "Where is this dark wizard? What happened to him?"

"He was punished. Suffering for eternity in some

hell of a netherworld. It's too good for him. I don't know which one."

"That makes no sense." Nostradamus swore softly. "What of the spell? What happened to the spell?"

I snarled and spat. *So that's what he was after.*

"Destroyed. Burned to ash," Morgan replied, smiling. "It was too dangerous."

Nostradamus sighed, sinking back against his chair. "So it's gone then." His expression crumpled into a downcast wad of dejection.

"No." Morgan's answer put a spark of hope back in his face. "Morgawse memorized it. She needed to save Mordred. Not that she ever found a way. Trying drove her mad. She had to be stopped."

Nostradamus grinned eagerly. "Do you know where she is? Where is your sister hiding?"

"Oh, yes. She's tucked away in some nameless netherworld past the outer reaches. A cozy little sleeping beauty. She'll never hurt anyone again."

"Which one?" Excitement oozed out his voice, the bastard.

"Some nameless thing. I never paid much attention."

I grinned. *Still careless with the intricacies of the netherworld, Morgan? Good. Let's hope you didn't tell him the rest of our little secret.*

Luckily, Nostradamus didn't press the issue.

"Unfortunate, but your sister is located past the outer reaches you said?"

"Yes."

"Then she shouldn't be too difficult to find." Nostradamus picked up his newspaper and rose. "You will wake up now and remember nothing of what transpired. All you will know is we had a lovely brunch but could not do business. And my face will fade from your memory over time."

He leaned forward again and whispered the end of the spell. "*Nidd ennyff llynnau.*"

Morgan came out of the spell and acted as if nothing had occurred. I watched them say their goodbyes and Nostradamus left. That's when I noticed the date of the newspaper. Two years ago.

I gasped. That was well before the blood sacrifice and our current mess.

"You lying bastard! What have you been up to?"

Then I felt the familiar shifting of the world and I was off.

I REMATERIALIZED in a hotel room.

Nostradamus sat in a chair by a window, poring over papers laid out on a small table. He muttered out loud. "I can find her. It will take time, but I can find her. I've explored the outer reaches. I know where to start."

I moved closer, trying to see his papers. I caught glimpses of maps and charts and long scrawling passages written in his own hand. I recognized bits of spells and more of his prophecies. The distinct quatrains could not be mistaken. I peered closer and noticed something odd. Another page of prophecies, but not in his usual style. I read the first prediction as he continued to ramble about finding Morgawse.

From Camelot
the exile comes

Corruption, chaos

from the blood of pain

To end the cycle

Nostradamus falls

"Well, shit, that makes no sense."

What does 'Nostradamus falls' mean? He can't die. A fall from grace?

I read on, finding a scrawled note underneath the first passage.

Blood magic? The end of magic? The end of me?

I shook my head and moved to the next prophecy.

Endings will bring Beginnings

In the game of kings and queens

and pawns will break fate

Seek him, seek him

The son of the dark witch

the hand of Camelot's end

He stands between the darkness

and the crown

He will turn the wheel

"What the hell gibberish is that!" I stared at Nostradamus. Then I noticed another scribbling at the end of the prophecy.

Why did the wizard use the spell on the boy? Why is this event important? Did something go wrong? Does this Mordred have the answer to my salvation? I don't want to die.

"Is this why you freed Morgawse? To find Mordred and save your own arse? How the bloody hell are they mixed up in this blood sacrifice mess?" I puffed out a breath of anger and disgust. "So much for your noble pursuit of 'saving magic'. You're just running scared." I smacked the back of Michel's head only to watch my hand pass right through him.

"What happened to you, Michel? You used to be more selfless, dedicated to helping people. Not causing trouble to save your own skin."

I turned away and welcomed the now familiar fade out of my surroundings.

Chapter Eighteen

Shadows

As the world coalesced back around me, I stood in the field where it had all started, facing Morgawse, Nostradamus, and Morgan, who was back among the conscious. Merlin's grimoire hovered above our heads, flapping its pages.

I glared at it. "This was all your doing, wasn't it?" The book flapped a page.

"What are you prattling about?" A roar came from Nostradamus. "What just happened? There was a flash of light, and you vanished. Now you've returned an instant later. What manner of tricks are you playing?"

"Not my tricks." I sneered at Nostradamus. "And

I'm not the liar, am I? Written any good prophecies lately?" I smiled as he blanched. I glanced at Morgawse and then Morgan before adding, "Maybe something regarding what *really* happened to Mordred."

The sisters gasped and I felt an immense satisfaction.

"Oh, yes. I know your little secrets. The things all of you have been hiding. The book there," I waved my hand at the grimoire, "took me on a trip down a few memory lanes." I inhaled, sensing the magic flowing through the earth under my feet. Energy flicked off my fingers and I shouted my next words, "Needless to say, I'm not in a good mood!"

"Nimue!" Morgan yelled and I faced her down, ready to blast her across the bloody countryside.

Until she said something I didn't expect.

"I'm sorry. I'm sorry I lied. But it was family. I was protecting family."

I took a breath to control my anger and shot back with my words not my magic. "Well, your 'family' has this wanker," I thumbed at Nostradamus, "all hot and bothered. Thinks Mordred is the key to saving his sorry hide from oblivion." I snorted. "That's the real reason he wants in on this fight. He thinks this darkness will end him somehow."

"You told me you wanted to save him!" Morgawse snarled and rammed her hands into Nostradamus' chest, knocking him off balance onto the grass. "You said if I helped you, told you the spell, you could save him! Bring him back!"

I chortled, short and harsh. "Whatever this charlatan told you, chances are he lied."

"I didn't lie." The protest from his lips sounded hollow. "Not precisely. Mordred's connected to all of this somehow. I'm not sure how yet. I need more time to decipher the visions."

Morgawse screeched. "You said you knew how to save him! You could use the wizard's spell."

Nostradamus snorted at Morgawse as he sat up. "I wanted that spell because I thought it was connected to the blood sacrifice. Perhaps an early attempt, but it was useless. Worthless to stop what is happening or to help your son."

Morgawse stood there, trembling.

Nostradamus seemed to take pity on her. "Perhaps I can yet fix what was done to Mordred, afterwards. Protecting magic must come first or all is lost."

"Oh please." I put my hands on my hips and stared at him with a look that would peel paint off a wall. "You're a lying louse and you're done. Leave this mess to me. All you're going to do is get up off your lying arse and take the four of us back to my cottage where we'll hash this out." I shifted my glare to Morgawse. "And you're going to shut up and cooperate. Or I swear I'll hunt down the both of you and turn you into crickets."

Nostradamus scrambled to his feet. I thought he'd fight, but he lowered his head, a hangdog look of contrition on his face. I didn't buy it for a minute but at least he was cooperating. I waited for Morgawse's response. She stared at her sister in silence, her face a stony impassive look of contempt.

Yet, she replied, "Fine."

"Then do your thing, Michel. Create a portal." As I kept an eye on Nostradamus and his magic, Morgan sidled up to me.

"I am sorry."

"I heard you the first time. This isn't over, and we will have words, but for now it's settled. We need to work together to get through this and figure out what's going on."

Morgan's lip quivered, but I refused to give her any more leniency. Instead, I marched over to the grimoire, intending to pluck it from the air. From the corner of my eye, I noticed the first edges of a portal forming.

As my hand reached up for the book, the strange smell of sweet cider drifted across the field and energy crackled off the breeze. I immediately looked at Nostradamus and Morgawse, but they weren't attacking. No portal had materialized, although the beginnings of the spell danced in the air. Morgawse backed away, staring at the ground, and Nostradamus looked puzzled. The skies darkened and a chilly wind blew across the grass.

My hand dropped. "What's wrong? What are you up to?" Tension and fear snapped out of my mouth.

"I am doing nothing untoward!" Nostradamus answered me with equal trepidation. "Yet, something is not right. The portal is not responding, something is interfering…"

In a sudden burst of light and magic, a force swept over the field and knocked all of us on our arses. A gateway appeared amid the beginnings of Nostradamus's portal, reeking of dark magic, and ice-cold air blasted out from its center. It coalesced into a swirling mass of thick inky mist and snapping red energy. Out of the vortex stepped a creature born of the same dark mist, all shadow and no substance with barely the form of a man.

It slithered through the air like a flying snake, with the speed of the wind, straight at Merlin's grimoire. I yelled like a banshee and scrambled to my feet, looking to head the thing off, but it never got close. With a piercing shriek, loud enough to wake the devil, the grimoire shot upward, spun around and disappeared in a flash of golden light. Leaving both me and the shadow creature staring at the open sky.

"Fuck!" I glared at the creature, so totally pissed off I didn't care if I was being reckless. "You bloody, gormless, piece of shit wanker! Look what you did!" I lunged at the thing, charging through it harmlessly, left only with a serious case of the shivers. "Fuck! And fuck again!"

The thing hissed at me. I slammed an energy ball at it, but it twisted its form; my attack slid through a hole in its vaporous body and smashed into a tree. It shot tendrils of shadows back at me. I dodged, and deflected them with magic shielding. Then I tossed a few luminous sparks of magic at it and the thing screeched as if in pain. It backed away from me, shifting back towards its portal, where it paused.

Nostradamus gaped at the thing, while Morgan grimaced, yelling, "What the hell is it?"

Then I saw Morgawse staring at it, almost as if she recognized it.

I raised a hand and that's when it happened. Black murky tendrils reached out like grotesque limbs, wrapped around Morgawse's waist and yanked her forward. Then she and the creature vanished through the portal.

"Bloody fucking hell and damnation!"

My words faded into Morgan's scream of rage and the sound of Nostradamus taking off across the field at a dead run. I watched him flee, the utter ridiculousness of the spectacle welling up inside me.

Morgan's voice cut across everything, dripping in anger and frustration, "Now what? Are we going to chase the bastard?"

I shoved the crazy urge to laugh down deep, and replied, "No. Let him go. We need to find out where the fuck we are and find a way home. Then figure out where the others went. Oh, and fucking track down the grimoire again!"

I ground my teeth. "We'll deal with him later."

Chapter Nineteen

Hunting Answers

After finding out we were near Lancaster, we took a short portal hop home. A damp Vivienne sat in my kitchen drinking tea and looking cross. A message was waiting on my answering machine from Iseult and Martin.

I played it back for everyone to hear. Iseult's voice echoed across the room.

"Letting you know we are all right. Don't know what happened but no injuries. Somehow Martin and I ended up by bloody Ipswich. I think there's a shortcut back but it may take an hour or so to arrange. Hope this gets to you."

The message ended and announced the time and date.

I glanced at the wall clock. "They left that an hour ago."

"Then if everything went well they should be here soon." Morgan poured herself a cup of tea and sat down near Vivienne. She asked her, "How did you get here?"

"I got dumped back in my lake, thank you very much. Swan-dived straight into the water. Not fun. May have ruined my new shoes. I left them outside to dry out." She raised a bare foot and wiggled her toes.

"You can thank Nostradamus for that," I added, "the bastard hijacked our portal."

"Oh, no. That's—Wait!" Vivienne turned her full attention on me. "Where's the grimoire? Don't tell me he snatched it?"

"No, that lovely piece of annoying literature took off on its own. Did a disappearing act when a shadow creature showed up."

"A shadow creature? What?"

A knock at the front door spared me any further explanations. I rose and left the kitchen for the entryway, then opened the door to see Martin and Iseult standing on my doorstep.

"You made it back in one piece. Wonderful. Come on

into the kitchen. We've made tea and were just about to start in with the explanations."

I ushered them inside, ignoring their questions until we were seated. Then we talked.

SEVERAL ARGUMENTS and explanations later—that included traipsing through Ipswich and a portal stone in Holywells Park—we sat in the garden drinking something stronger than tea. My anger at all the lies still simmered, but I was being civil. There were more important things to deal with than my wounded pride.

"So, the way I see it," I took a soothing sip of mead and continued, "the most pressing issue is to track down the grimoire again, before Nostradamus, and find a way to undo the blood sacrifice spell."

"How do we know this isn't a wild-goose chase? That the grimoire can even help?" Iseult downed a swig of gin after asking the question. Her haggard expression spoke volumes.

I sipped some mead and stifled a yawn. Staying up all night was harder than it used to be. "We don't for certain, but we know Merlin created some version of the blood sacrifice spell. And he never created anything he couldn't undo. So it stands to reason there's a reversal spell in the grimoire." I leaned back in my chair. "It's our best hope for putting an end to whatever plan this dark shadowy evil has concocted."

"What about my sister?" I tried not to bristle at the sound of Morgan's voice. "We need to rescue her. I know she may not deserve our help, but we just can't leave her in the clutches of that shadow creature."

My hand tightened over the arm of the chair. "I doubt she needs rescuing. She recognized the shadow that tried to steal the grimoire. I don't know how but she knew the creature. And it singled her out among all of us so I think it knew her as well."

Morgan fidgeted. "But that doesn't mean she's safe."

I shook my head, casting her a sympathetic look. "Doesn't it? Morgawse has had lifetimes of allying herself with disreputable people. You know as well as I that she'll switch sides in a heartbeat. I'm betting the shadow worked for the dark wizard I met, and Morgawse is now siding with him against us." At Morgan's frown, I added, "Besides, the best way to help her, on the off chance she isn't siding with evil, is to find the grimoire."

Morgan crossed her arms, but didn't argue.

"Do you know how to track down the book?" Vivienne's voice drifted out into the air, followed by a slight aroma of summer lake water. I glanced over. She was glowing.

"Shit!" I thumped down my half-consumed glass of mead. "We have incoming!"

Vivienne's body stiffened as her skin glowed blue, the colour of a summer sky. Her eyes rolled, turning opaque white and stared blankly into space. Her voice sounded a deep, harsh hiss before she spoke.

"*The drums of destiny are sounding. For the end. For the beginning. The Dark King comes against the Rise of the Queen. The prophet falls to the Queen's hand. Sacrifice for sacrifice. Seek the past. Seek the memory. The pages will unfold. Secrets will surface.*"

Vivienne slumped back in her chair, dazed and semi-conscious, the magic and visions vanishing.

I took a breath, exhaled, and grabbed my glass of mead. I took a long, slow drink, wishing to hell I was back in bed. I replied to Vivienne's original question as if nothing had happened, while Iseult flapped around Viv, trying to revive her. "I do know how to track down the grimoire. And I think her vision just confirmed my suspicions of where it went."

"Really?" Morgan scoffed. "You're just going to ignore that rant about kings and queens? What if it's important? What if it's about Gwenevere?"

"Fuck Gwenevere, I don't care. The grimoire is what's important." They glared at me. I took another drink and glared back. "I think the damn thing went back to Merlin's Sanctum. I can work a spell to confirm; that won't be the hard part. Getting to the blasted book will be the trick." I finished my glass of mead and set it down on the table with a satisfying clink.

"I went back after our wanker wizard escaped the cave and I, well, trapped him again." I waved at Merlin the tree. "The place is still sealed off. I never did figure out how Elaine freed him; Martin showed me the spell they used, but it shouldn't have worked. Must have been a glitch somewhere that let Merlin out but left the shielding up. I sure as hell never got back inside to investigate." I shrugged. "Maybe when Mark originally stole the book, something in the spell changed. I'll have to do more research."

"How did Mark steal the book?" Martin asked. "It took me forever to even get close to breaching your spell, and even then it felt odd."

I glanced over at him, huddled in his chair, arms crossed. His hand kept touching his throat. "Mark used Merlin's own retrieval spell. I don't know how he got his hands on it, but he didn't have to get through my magic barrier. The book came to him. My magic wouldn't contain the grimoire if it wanted to leave. Or return home."

Martin sucked in his breath. "Can't we do that again?"

"Would that we could, but I don't know the spell. And unless you fancy another trip to see Mark, that solution is off the table."

Martin looked at his grandmother and shook his head.

I leaned back in my chair with a smirk, as Vivienne's eyes fluttered open. "So that's the gist, ladies and gent. Once I confirm the grimoire's whereabouts, we need to break into Merlin's sanctum."

I poured myself another glass of mead as a confused Vivienne asked, "What did I miss?"

AFTER A quick nap to refresh, I sat alone in the garden and prepared the spell circle, the ingredients in a box beside me. Everyone else stayed inside, sulking, or mad, or too timid to venture out. I didn't blame them; I was in a bear of a mood.

My circle was made of sand, from the edge of Vivienne's lake, and inside I placed—at five points along the rim—an acorn, a pinch of ash from a burned yew branch, a sprig of rowan, an ivy leaf, and a small piece of Merlin's blackthorn bush.

"Let the magic touch the fire." I snapped my fingers and small sparks of green magic danced around the piece of Merlin, before snaking across the ground to connect to the ash of the yew.

"Bring the oak, for the power." The magic wriggled across to tether to the acorn.

"For protection, awaken the rowan." A thread slid over to join in the rowan sprig.

"To close the circle and bind the worlds." The thread brought in the last element and the circle erupted in a flash of green light. It shimmered and wavered.

"Find the one whose magic resonates among the blackthorn. Find me Merlin's grimoire."

Rings spread across the emerald shimmer like ripples in a pond, then the light faded into a vision. A scene of a dark cave interior, still full of scorched walls, damaged furniture and shattered glass. Merlin's Sanctum.

And there, laying on the floor amidst the debris, was the grimoire.

I peered into the otherworldly window, trying to see any clue, any sign of how Merlin escaped or a way in, but I found nothing. I let the magic fade, and with an angry wipe of my hand I swept away part of the sand circle and other bits of the spell. I stared down at the mess I made and chewed on my lip.

Then I scooped the acorn and rowan back into the box. The ivy leaf had crumbled so I smeared it and the sand into the earth, covering it with dirt. I ground Merlin's blackthorn into the soil with the heel of my shoe. I picked up the box, rose to my feet, and went back inside.

I heard voices from the parlour but avoided them, heading instead to my storage pantry where I tucked away the box. I slipped out and snuck upstairs. I stole unnoticed into my bedroom and shut the door.

There I lay down on the bed and had a good cry.

After my emotional breakdown, I went to the en-suite, splashed some cold water on my face and tidied myself up. I left the bedroom and met Morgan as I was coming downstairs.

"I thought you were in the garden?" she asked.

"I was." The words were brusque to cover the hoarseness in my voice. "I finished the spell. I came up here to think for a few minutes. Mull things over."

"Okay. Did you come up with any ideas?"

"Not yet. But I did confirm the grimoire is in Merlin's sanctum. I was just coming down to tell everyone."

"Everyone's in the parlour. Vivienne's still feeling a bit chilly and I'm fetching her a blanket. I'll meet you back there."

"Yeah. She gets like that sometimes." I couldn't

keep the wistful sadness out of my voice and I turned away before Morgan could ask any questions. I moved past her, descending. Her footsteps faded away and I paused when I reached the bottom step.

I glanced towards the parlour and then at the door to the garden. I could walk out and never look back. Let it all crumble, get swallowed by whatever was coming. Turn a blind eye and let it be consumed, let it all burn. I felt like it. I wanted to, just walk out and abandon everything. Then I stepped onto the floor and headed to the parlour.

TWO HOURS later we still had no answers but I managed to fix the equilibrium of the group by plying Iseult with chocolate, Morgan with wine, and Vivienne with whisky-laced tea. Martin was just glad we weren't grumbling and sniping at each other anymore.

I let the others talk amongst themselves as I closed my eyes and let my mind drift. I let my thoughts wander back to the day that Merlin reappeared on my doorstep. Did he leave any clues in what he said? Any remarks, any gestures, any stray bits of magic clinging to his clothing? But I could remember none. I let my mind float in the sea of memory, trying to grasp any random synapses that could lead me to a clue, lead me inside Merlin's sanctum.

All that happened was I fell asleep.

The next thing I knew, Morgan shook me awake.

"Wake up. I think Martin may have stumbled on the answer."

"What?" I blinked several times. "What happened?"

"Burnt caramel." Martin's tongue tumbled over the words in a rush to get them out. I gaped at him, confused.

"Do you remember when I singed Merlin?" I nodded. "Well, um, I told them about that and I mentioned that when he, um, caught on fire, um, he smelled like burnt caramel."

Morgan butted into the conversation. "Do you remember Budapest?"

"I do. What does that have to do with... oh, burnt caramel." The connection finally clicked. "That wily little trickster and his spell to escape the Fae. Yeah, the whole place smelled like burnt caramel afterwards. And it lingered for days." I pursed my lips. "So what's your theory?"

Morgan nudged Martin. "Tell her."

"Well," Martin fumbled over the word, before blurting, "We think Elaine may have used something similar to help Merlin escape. She was in another room when I cast the spell, and the whole casting seemed *directed*. At the time, I thought it was the way it worked, but now…"

"Interesting. So you think she combined that escape spell with yours, breached the sanctum, and pulled Merlin out?" I tapped the arm of my chair with a finger. "Could be. That might have worked. And the after effects of *her* magic got caught up in *my* spell."

They nodded and I fell silent for a minute, musing. "It might be a solution. I think the Budapest spell was called the Nomad's Light. I may have something like that in one of my books."

I looked up and saw Martin's smiling face. At least his mind was off what had happened in Annwn. "Go fetch me the Labyrinth Compendium. I think that's where I saw it."

Martin ran off like a rabbit and returned post-haste with the book.

I flipped through the index pages until I found what I

sought, turning to the spell. "Here it is." I did a quick read, a shiver of delight running through me. "Shit. This could work. Combine it with a reversal of Martin's spell and it could allow us to slip right through the seal."

"Okay," Iseult's exasperated voice broke in. "Can we stop the pretense and explain something to me? If you cast the spell, how come you simply can't uncast it or break it? Why do we need all this rigmarole and some other spell? That makes no sense to me."

"The spell that imprisoned Merlin became autonomous the moment it was cast." I paused when a flicker of memory surfaced. I stuffed it back down. "It's self sustaining and self-replicating. It can't be broken. Not by me or anyone else. It was supposed to hold Merlin forever."

"Well, that worked out, didn't it?" Iseult snorted and fell silent, slumping back in her chair.

I ignored the jibe and closed the spellbook. "Well, we have a plan. On to Merlin's Sanctum next."

Chapter Twenty

The Grimoire

The violet glow of the barrier spell illuminated the interior of the cavern and cast an eerie glimmer on the ruins of Merlin's sanctum. A faint hum filled the space where we stood, mixed with a *drip, drip* of water from somewhere. I smelled dirt and mould, with a hint of ozone. My hand tightened on the strap of my satchel.

I took a deep breath. I hated this place.

Beside me, I heard Morgan's nervous breathing. She had insisted on coming with me. I didn't like it but the spells needed two people and she was the best choice.

So much of this could go horribly wrong. If I made one error in adjusting the intent of the spells... I don't want to end up trapped here forever. Or lost in–between worlds.

"Bloody hell." My anxiety came out in a whisper. "No use wishing or standing here." I rummaged inside my bag and pulled out two potion bottles, handing one to Morgan. "Drink up. Better to get this over with quick, whatever happens."

"Way to boost the morale there." Morgan grabbed the bottle and downed the potion. I did the same.

Nomad's Light bent reality and folded dimensions. The potions prepared us for the shift so our bodies wouldn't implode or something equally dire. Martin's spell should weaken the barrier long enough for us to slip through and not bounce off.

Hopefully I haven't screwed up the spell combination.

My skin tingled as I fished out copies of the combined spells from my satchel; a sign the potions were working. I handed Morgan her part of the spell-working and we waited.

After a minute, our skin glowed a pale green and the air turned to bright flashing colours; all pastel blues and yellows. The rocks and walls of the cavern shifted into geometrical lines and shapes and slid against each other like fault lines. I looked at the barrier and saw slivers and gaps between its strands of energy.

"Okay, it seems to be working. You feeling all right, Morgan?"

She clenched her jaw. "Oh, just grand."

I nodded and stared at my part of the spell. Blinking to focus my vision, I read the modified incantation aloud, "Between the cracks, around the barriers, we move. As wind, as air, as spirits, we are set free. Through the obstacles, past the locks, we find the way. Show us the path." Then I nodded at Morgan.

She cleared her throat and intoned, "Walk the worlds of in-between, along the cracks betwixt reality. Shift the paths of here and there and open the folds of actuality. Drift existence, merge your substance, and move within the rifts."

As her last word faded, the air crackled in sparks, a web of energy flashing past our eyes and merging with the sanctum shielding. Both of us held our breath as a spinning wheel of light slowly materialized. We moved forward and a sudden burst of power hit the both of us like a ton of bricks.

Every atom in my body burst in fiery pain and

dissolved, and then flattened like cardboard. I didn't have time to scream before every sensation in my body shut off, and I was yanked forward.

Then I stared at the ceiling inside Merlin's sanctum. I felt the rocky floor dig into my back and I groaned in pain. An answering groan came from Morgan.

"Fuck," she whispered. "And we have to do that again to get out."

I swore, and exhaled a breath. I slowly rose to my knees, trying not to vomit. I crawled over to the grimoire and stuffed it into my satchel.

"I got the grimoire. Let's get this damn trip over with and leave."

"Fuck," Morgan swore again. "Fine, do it."

Gritting our teeth we said the spells again, and seconds later we were out and groaning on the cavern floor. This time I did vomit, spewing my lunch over a flat bit of rock. Behind me, Morgan did the same.

Once our equilibrium and our stomachs had settled, we hiked out of the cavern without trouble. As we exited into the fresh air of Somerset, we paused for another rest and I caught Morgan staring at me.

"Did I bollocks things up between us for good?" Morgan asked. "You're my best friend. Did I ruin that with my lying about Mordred?"

"No." I paused, trying to order my thoughts. "I'm mad, sure, but I'll get over it. It's not just you. Things happened after Nostradamus hijacked our portals, secrets came out. Memories. I was hurt and upset about more than you. Besides..." I stopped, suddenly realizing I hadn't told her about what Nostradamus had done to her in France. "Something else I witnessed. We need to talk about it and you're not going to like it. But not here." I glanced back at the tunnel caves as wind blew at my hair. I shivered.

Then I turned back and saw the confusion in Morgan's eyes. "We're good, Morgan. Mostly. The rest will smooth over in time. But we do need to..." A loud rumble interrupted any further explanations.

"What the hell?" I yelled as light streaked across the sky and a screeching noise shattered the peaceful countryside. The familiar hum and flash of a portal appeared and Nostradamus walked out of the cave entrance.

"Shit!" This time Morgan swore.

Both of us moved together, on the attack, but Nostradamus was quicker, conjuring a strange shimmering box. He threw the spell at us and it exploded in a shower of dust and sparks. He laughed and shouted, "You are *my* prisoners now."

And then we were gone.

When the magic faded, both Morgan and I stood in a dark space. I tentatively reached out a hand and felt a smooth surface under my fingers. I reached out in another direction and felt the same surface.

"Shit!" My heart sunk as I recognized our confinement. "We're in an Obsidian Box."

"Can't we get a damn break?" Morgan screamed in frustration for both of us. "Curse that damn bastard." She pounded her fist against a wall. "Bollocks! So we're stuck here until that knob decides to let us out?"

I nodded. "Or he just shows up and takes the book, leaving us to rot." My jaw clenched and my stomach churned again. I pulled my satchel closer, tightening my grip on the bag.

Then I realized my fingers were glowing. Faint, but a definite glow.

"The spell is still working!" I dug in my satchel and pulled out the incantations. "That's our way home."

Morgan moaned, but we read the spells again, and sure enough, the magic folded us inside out and yanked us out of Nostradamus' prison. Unfortunately, we encountered a shower of dark corrupted sparks mid-shift and everything went to hell.

The spell short-circuited. We screamed as the atomic folding reversed and we reverted to normal. With every nerve in agony, we fell out of two-dimensional space and dropped down into the twisting netherworld vortex.

We plummeted along the interconnected web of worlds. Sliding and bouncing between the realities and illusions, smashing through all the walls and barriers, our free fall ricocheted us like a pinball in an arcade machine. We were finally spit out in some nameless speck of a netherworld and we rolled to a stop in a flurry of bruises and scrapes.

"Well, that was not fun." Morgan sat up and spit out dirt and some bile.

I remained sprawled on my back, still clutching my satchel and my stomach. "At least we're away from Nostradamus."

"How the hell did he even find us in the first place?"

"Maybe he's tracking us somehow. The bastard's clever." I finally sat up, fighting nausea, a pain in my head, and a twinge in my spine. "Speaking of which, let's go home before he shows up again."

Morgan snorted, "If he can track what we just did, he's not a wizard, he's a miracle worker."

"Hopefully he can't." I reached in my satchel for the powder to spell a new portal and go home. "Shit! It's gone!"

"What?" Morgan stared, confused, then, "Not the portal dust?"

I nodded, a morose feeling creeping around my brain. "It may have fallen out during our tumble." I tightened my arms around my bag.

"Check again. Maybe you missed it." Fear snaked out with her words.

I tucked the grimoire in my lap and took the satchel off my shoulder, dumping the contents out onto the gravelly surface of the netherworld. No container of portal dust. "See. It's gone." I stared at the jumbled heap of items, all useless to get us home.

"Well, I'm not getting stuck here!" Morgan scrambled to her feet. "We'll scope this place out or… Wait. You've got that damn grimoire. That's got to have a way to get home in it somewhere."

I continued to stare at the pile from my satchel. "Doubtful. Merlin liked prepared spells, we'll never—"

"Dammit! Just look! Better than sitting here brooding or whatever you're doing. Besides, that damn book has a mind of its own. I doubt it wants to be stuck here anymore than we do."

With a sigh, I dumped my items back in the bag. Morgan was right. Doing something was better than wallowing. I sat crossed legged and opened the book on my lap, turning to the index. I ran a finger along the edge of the page and felt a corresponding tingle under my fingertip.

"Show us how to get home."

The book glowed, its pages fluttering, before flying from my grasp as if yanked by an unseen hand.

"What the hell?"

It spun in the air, a musical harmony filling the space.

Morgan put a hand on my shoulder. "Is that tune…"

"Greensleeves? Yeah, I think it is." I looked up to see Morgan shake her head.

"Did that book conk its noggin during our trip? Why the fuck is it spinning like a top and playing some damn folk tune?"

I shrugged. "I have no idea. But the grimoire always behaves with a purpose. Just wait for it."

No sooner than the words were out of my mouth, than the message appeared on a wall.

From harmony, the summoning. Companions to fetch you home. But first, she will come for you.

Before I could fathom the meaning, the book stopped spinning, snapped shut and shot back into my hands. I felt a surge of magic and, in an instant, I was somewhere else.

Chapter Twenty-One

The Lady

One minute I sat in a netherworld, the next I stood in an empty ballroom, Victorian by the look of the architecture. The solid sense of the grimoire in my arms was the only thing that felt real. I closed my eyes for a moment, tired of being batted around like a ping-pong ball and being a pawn in someone else's game. My patience was at an end.

I opened my eyes and shouted, "I don't care who you are or what elaborate charade you're playing at, show yourself now, or I'll rip this world apart until I find you!"

"No need for that. I just brought you here for a chat." A lyrical, melodic voice drifted out of the ether. A female form glimmered into existence, wearing a blue silk gown with capped sleeves. Long white gloves covered her hands and a feathered black mask concealed her face.

I snorted. "What? Playing at a fancy masquerade?"

She laughed. "Indulge me. I'm not ready to reveal my secrets to you. Not yet. It might… influence things."

"So what are you ready to reveal? A name maybe?" I tapped my foot as I waited.

She straightened her shoulders and lifted her chin. "I am called the Lady."

"Thought so." I crossed my arms. "Mark thinks highly of you, but I'm not quite so impressed."

She moved a few steps closer, the skirt of her gown swishing against the tiled floor. "I didn't expect you would be. You're not one to impress easily. Or trust in the word of another. You need reasons."

She moved closer, but I didn't retreat. Instead, I moved toward her until we were inches apart. "Yeah, I do. I don't trust because I've been burned too many times by too many people, and I'm not impressed because I know that people lie and manipulate. So show me why you're worth trusting. That you turned a selfish louse like Mark around with truth and not some scam. Because on this side of the game board it seems like you're a cheat."

Her lips stopped smiling and her eyes narrowed. "Sometimes you have to cheat to win. You know that better than anyone. Swallow your pride and your injured feelings and listen. I have to stay one step ahead to even have a chance of winning. If that means manipulation, subterfuge and hiding out within the shadows to protect the worlds, then so be it. I'm not ashamed, and I'm not backing down. If you can't handle that, then maybe you aren't the person we need."

For a heartbeat I paused, then nodded. "Very good. I'll give you points for passion. And I'll listen. Why did you drag me here?"

"Two reasons. I want to give you a gift." A small silver box suddenly materialized on her outstretched hand. "Take it."

I plucked the box from her fingers and then hesitantly opened it. Inside lay a pygmy dragon's claw. I gasped. Those things were rare and powerful. "And this is for?"

"You'll see." She grinned.

Irritated, I asked brusquely, "What's the second reason?"

"To warn you. You'll have difficult decisions to make in the days ahead and another secret will surface someday soon. Dark days are on the horizon. Something you won't expect is coming and will be very heart-breaking. I need you to be strong and—" She stopped abruptly, as if she sensed something else. "You have to go back now! Be prepared for a fight."

Light flashed and I was suddenly gone from the ballroom and back in the netherworld in the middle of a fight. Iseult and Morgan traded magic blows with Nostradamus and behind them gleamed an open portal door.

I shoved the silver box into my satchel and tucked the grimoire under my arm. Then I slammed a magic energy ball right into the bastard's chest, sending Nostradamus flying backward. I rushed forward and pushed Morgan and Iseult through his portal and jumped in after them.

Chapter Twenty-Two

The Chase

"Move, move. That bastard will be right behind us." Barely glancing at my surroundings, other than to notice that we had landed in yet another cavernous netherworld, I urged the others to run. I looked back seeing the portal snap shut, buying us a little more time. Then we all took off down the nearest tunnel.

A dozen twists and turns later, we were reasonably sure we had a respite from our continued pursuer and all-round wanker of a wizard.

As we caught our collected breath, I grabbed Iseult's arm. "Tell me you have portal dust?"

She nodded, waving a bottle. "From your stores

cupboard in the pantry."

"Good." I pulled an empty flask from a satchel pocket and snatched the other bottle from Iseult. I hastily poured some dust into the empty container and handled the rest back to her. "We need to split up. You and Morgan take off to the left," I nodded at a tunnel, "and high-tail it home."

"Where are you going?"

"The grimoire and I are going to play cat-and-mouse with a bastard."

"The grimoire?" Morgan frowned. "Are you mad? What if he catches you?"

I grinned. "You can't set a trap without good bait. Now get going, and off to somewhere safe."

They took off down the left side tunnel and I raced away in the opposite direction. Somehow I knew in my bones Nostradamus was coming, and I suspected it was the grimoire he was tracking, at least this time. He had held it long enough to get a feel for its magic and it wouldn't be hard for a wizard of his skill to track a magic signature. That meant leading him away from the others and turning the tables.

The problem was a lack of resources. The empty, shoddy bit of a netherworld where we had landed wasn't much more than a rocky labyrinth; I had to find a better place. That meant some world hopping. So with a tiny pinch of dust and a wish I crossed my fingers and moved on. Hits one and two were a miss—the first one being occupied with angry elves and the second home to very large spiders—and Nostradamus caught up with me on number three.

The bastard was waiting for me when I landed. How he had anticipated my arrival was a mystery. I'm betting he just got lucky.

His face was a mask of fury and frustration. "Enough of these foolish games!" His roar shook the moss on this netherworld's trees and rattled its hanging ivy. "I grow weary of chasing you like a hound after a stag. Give me the grimoire!"

I reached into my bag to the pocket where I always kept a special treat, my hand closing on a stiff paper packet. "Have you ever been to Bonfire Night?"

He gaped, his mouth open, giving him a slight resemblance to a dead fish. "You are mad." He reached out his hand, repeating, "Give me the grimoire."

I shifted my stance, preparing. I grinned, ignoring his demands. "It's all about the fireworks."

And then I lobbed the prepared spell directly at his head. The packet erupted on impact and he screamed as a thousand tiny explosions detonated across his face. As he danced in pain, I jumped through a hastily conjured portal.

Two more jumps and I was running out of dust, but I finally found a suitable world. A bright, beautiful realm, quiet and empty, but with just the right vegetation and plant life. A few choice ingredients here, scrawled runes in the dirt, with a few old glyphs, and beating my own record for spell preparation, brought me right under the wire for Nostradamus' arrival.

As he portalled in, I stood in the centre of three concentric rings, each created from symbols and earth, woven with powerful plant-based charms. Strong protection against any type of magic, but with a special surprise built in for my old friend.

The portal faded and he stood outside the circles. His face was badly singed and one eye was swollen. Anger radiated off his expression and he scowled like he wanted to boil me alive. Our eyes locked. Memories bloomed and dissolved, and we solidified as enemies.

He spoke first. "It didn't have to be this way. You could have stepped aside. Let me handle what must be done."

I smirked. "Because only the great Nostradamus is capable of such a feat?" I barked a short derisive laugh. "Well, I have news for you. You're the *only one* who thinks you can handle breaking the spell." I crossed my arms and sneered. "No one wants you or your ego."

"And who are you to talk of ego? You stand there in defiance, insulting me, pretending you are the witch for the job." He spat. "Hah! You have not the will nor the skill."

"You have no idea what I have. Even when we were together. I learned that lesson early. Never show your full hand to a man, especially if he is a wizard."

His lips narrowed into a thin, grim-looking line. "It would be like you to hide things. You never trust fully, do you?" His every word was laced in judgement.

"No. But it's funny, you judging me about secrets. Your heart is full of them. Wrapped up in all that fear you carry about your end." I tilted my head studying him. "Is that why you pursued wizardry? To beat death? I always thought it was for the knowledge, to feed your mind, but now I wonder."

"Why not? I saw enough of it in France. Felt its effects in my heart as my family was lost to the grave. Why shouldn't I shun it? I know you cannot understand, not with your longing for the company of the reaper. Unlike you, I welcomed eternal life."

"You had a choice. I didn't. There lies the difference." I watched a flicker in his eyes. A twinge of guilt perhaps, or understanding. Or maybe contempt. I couldn't tell anymore. "That's changed, though, hasn't it? Your choice is slipping out of your grasp. Death is coming for you. Isn't that what you fear?"

He inhaled a hiss of breath and moved forward, to the edge of the circle. "Is that your plan? Try to anger me enough that I would step in your trap? I am too clever. I know these circles, and I will not step within them. I do not need to." He stared down at my magic workings and began to chant. His fingers danced with his power and he began to weave his spell into mine.

I whispered, "I know you're clever. Too clever for your own good. And you used to be more subtle. Luckily for me, you've changed."

I closed my eyes as the magic of my working flowed from the earth, running through the circles and merging with Nostradamus' power. "Gotcha." I swallowed and said the last words of my spell. "*Newyeich lwych, newyeich llech.*"

When I opened my eyes I looked at Nostradamus from outside the rings. He stood in the middle of the center ring, trapped inside by his own magic and mine. I waved as he let out a scream of rage.

"This will not hold me forever! I will break free and come for you! Come for the grimoire!"

I shrugged. "I know, but it might hold you long enough for me to use the grimoire and clean up this mess. And it will certainly hold you long enough for me to get home in peace without you chasing me down."

I used the last of the portal dust to toddle off to my cottage, leaving a still screaming Nostradamus behind.

Chapter Twenty-Three

Spells and Revelations

I portalled home to anxious faces and spell paraphernalia; apparently everyone had been trying to find me. I might have been truly touched if they hadn't made a bloody mess of my garden.

I growled at Martin. "Go fetch my silver bowl, the bag of hazel bark, two fox bones and a raven feather." As he scurried off, I shouted after him, "And some whisky."

"Hard day?" Morgan smirked at me. "And hello, glad you survived our current wanker wizard. Is he on ice?"

"For now. But I still have to disguise the grimoire. I think the bastard was tracking it. Best to be safe."

"Oh. That's what those things are for." Iseult chimed

in and I shot her a quizzical look. She shrugged. "I cast a few hiding spells in my day, to cover my tracks from Tristan and Mark." She gave me a shy smile. "Interesting choice of a binder, though, and adding the bones. I usually went with gin and oak bark."

"I need something older and with more flexibility to hide the book's magic from prying eyes. Whisky has a long history and foxes have a connection to tricksters."

"Ah. That makes sense."

At that point Martin rushed back into the garden out of breath with the supplies. He plunked everything I asked for in a jumble on the nearest table and sat down, puffing like he had run a marathon. I really was going to have to talk to him about exercising better.

I cleared off another table and placed the grimoire down. I patted the cover, for my reassurance or its, I wasn't sure. The others made themselves comfortable and watched as I worked. In the silver bowl, I poured a generous amount of whisky, then took a quick swallow from the bottle for me. I added a good dollop of the hazel bark, and the fox bones, stirring it all with the raven feather. Then I chanted the incantation.

"Through the water of life, feel the bones shift. Through the bones' decay flows the change. Through the change comes the dream. Through the dream flows the reality into the raven. From the raven reality transforms."

The mixture in the silver bowl glittered in a soft white light and I dipped the raven feather into the bowl. The magic danced along the feather fusing into its essence. I brushed the plumage against the leather of the book and painted it in the cloaking spell. The grimoire glowed in sparkles of white that faded after a few minutes. It also smelled vaguely of whisky.

I placed a hand on the book. No sense of its magic radiated outward, but I could still feel its heart. I had done enough, though, to stop any tracking spell.

"It worked." I set aside the bowl after plucking out the fox bones and giving them a shake. I set them to one side with the feather to dry and picked up the whisky bottle.

I turned to everyone and announced, "The grimoire may be protected, but we can't stay here. It's the first place Nostradamus and Morgawse will come looking. Any suggestions on where we can hide out?"

Morgan crossed her legs. "My place is out. My sister knows it. Wouldn't wonder if that wizard knows too."

"It's a good bet," I agreed. "In fact, we should rule out any place associated with you."

Morgan frowned. "Why?"

"I'll tell you later." I wasn't looking forward to that conversation, and turned to Iseult to forestall any more questions. "Do you know somewhere?"

Iseult shook her head. "Most of my hideouts were compromised, and I doubt a netherworld is safe."

Which probably left Vivienne out of the mix, but I looked at her all the same. She just shrugged. Then a voice piped up behind me.

"I might know a place."

I turned to see Martin looking sheepish. "An old mate of mine, down in London, he owns this place. Rents it out. But I know for a fact it's empty at the moment. He's thinking of selling, so no tenants. But he hasn't started showing it yet, so it's not likely anyone would come by."

I nodded. "Sounds like as good a place as any. Pack

up, people, we're headed to London."

THE PLACE Martin led us turned out to be a cozy little Victorian era townhouse. He cleared it with his mate, so we moved in on the up and up and not by sneaking around for once. I was a bit surprised by his stepping up, but Martin did have his layers. He usually liked to keep his personal life private; all I knew about him was he had run with an artistic crowd in London and that he had a crush on the bloke who worked at the local post office.

I threw my gear in a ground floor bedroom before settling in the lounge area with the grimoire. The others excused themselves; Vivienne and Martin headed to the kitchen, with Morgan and Iseult disappearing into the bedrooms they had claimed for themselves. I welcomed the solitude; a bit of peace and quiet to study the grimoire.

Half past the hour, Morgan brought me some supper. I set the book down and accepted a plate of takeaway chicken curry and a roll. The smell made my mouth water and I tucked into it with gusto.

Morgan sat in an armchair across from me. "Have you found anything yet?"

I shook my head and replied between mouthfuls of food, "Nothing about his blood sacrifice spell. Plenty of other interesting things, though. Whatever else he was, Merlin did know his stuff. All formal intricate spellwork, but very innovative in its own way." I licked a fleck of curry off the corner of my lip. "It may take a while yet. There are hundreds of spells in the pages, and some of them shift as you read. Others disappear or appear out of the blue. Merlin liked to keep his secrets."

"Okay, I'll leave you to it then." Morgan rose. "The rest of us are going to do some research of our own. Look through some of the books we brought to see if we can't find some mention of that shadow creature that snatched my sister. Might give us a lead on the wizard behind this as well."

I looked up from my plate, raising an eyebrow. "Good idea. Any information might help us stop what's happening and put things to rights."

She nodded and left the room, and I went back to finishing my supper.

After I cleaned the plate and sopped up the curry sauce with the bread, I set it aside. I wiped my hands with a napkin and a touch of magic, and returned to reading the grimoire. An hour in, after two different treatises on time manipulation, thirty-seven spells on glamours and illusions, one about turning vinegar into wine—which I bookmarked—and a two-page cure for warts, I closed my eyes for a break.

I took calming breaths to relax and let my frustration ease. I felt a tingle under my fingertips, where they touched the pages of the grimoire, a familiar sensation of magic. My eyes shot open in an instant of panic.

I wasn't in the lounge anymore. I was back in Merlin's sanctum. Back in my memory. He was by his table, the other me was slumped on the floor, and all the spell ingredients were spread out, ready to prepare. Yet, everything was frozen; a suspended moment in time.

I moved closer, despite my desire to shut my eyes and wish myself away. I touched the edge of that fateful spell that burned through my heart, pushing at the edge of the first sheet of vellum. Then I noticed something, scribbling that hadn't been there when Merlin first revealed his plan to me.

His handwriting, just a few words scrawled in Latin, "Arthur was a dangerous mistake. Must start again."

I frowned, puzzled over the meaning, but had no time to contemplate as the memory suddenly shifted into motion as if someone had flipped a switch. I stepped back, watching Merlin prepare the spell, and then turn to me. I forced myself to watch this time, as I knocked him into the table, and the spell exploded. I watched myself flee and Merlin fall, caught in the blast, as the cave erupted in a burst of unrestrained magic.

The dust settled, and I stared at an unconscious Merlin sprawled in the debris. I knew what would come next. Eventually I would return and find him unconscious, in a magical coma, undone by his own unwillingness to let go.

Except… that's not what happened next.

Merlin groaned. The bastard was waking up.

"What the fuck!"

My shout echoed around the recreated moment in time as Merlin opened his eyes. He lifted himself up onto an elbow, holding his head, which bled from a cut. Movement caught my eye, and someone else stepped out of the shadows.

A dark cloaked figure, not much more than a silhouette.

He's using a masking spell? What's going on?

The man moved around the table, his hand brushing against Merlin's spell. He flicked his fingers, energy sparked, and the vellum turned to ash.

I gasped. I remembered seeing those ashes when I returned. I always thought the spell had burned in the magical backlash. I stared as he moved forward, attacking an unsuspecting Merlin, grabbing him around the throat. I heard indistinct murmurs from the man as Merlin clawed at the dark fingers holding him by the neck, unsuccessfully trying to scream.

Within a few seconds, Merlin slumped back into unconsciousness and the dark figure let him go. A noise distracted my attention, and my other self returned to the sanctum. When I glanced back, Merlin was as I found him that day and the dark figure had disappeared.

Then the memory faded and I was back in my chair in the sitting room, the grimoire still in my lap. My hands shook. Everything I thought I knew was wrong. All these centuries, I had been wrong. In the aftermath of my emotions and guilt,

I had inadvertently covered up the truth.

The memories of the rest of that day came flooding back. My finding Merlin, dragging his unconscious body farther into the cave and making a makeshift pallet for him to spend his eternal rest. Then leaving, and sealing up his sanctum to any and all trespassers with the self-regenerating spell.

Shit! I let the creature truly responsible for Merlin's condition get away.

As I sat, my mind whirling in overwhelming revelations, the grimoire moved against my hand. I jerked my fingers and the pages flipped rapidly on their own. About three quarters of the way through the book, the movement stopped and the grimoire settled down. I looked at the page, and staring back at me was Merlin's blood sacrifice spell and the way to reverse it.

"Well, shit. All that time searching and now you decide to show it." I studied the page, seeing a mixture of Latin, and of all things, the spellwork version of ogham. "I'll have to translate that."

I hefted the book and got to my feet, heading for

the kitchen. I also stuffed all my emotions off into a dark corner of my mind. I'd have to sort them later, but more important things first.

"Morgan!" I shouted as I burst into the kitchen, "Did we bring that copy of Doirend's grimoire with us?" Four guilty faces looked up from bowls of ice cream.

Morgan put down her spoon. "Yeah, but I think I left it upstairs. You find something?"

I turned the book around so they could see the page. "I found a possible way to reverse the spell. But it needs to be translated." I moved to the nearby table and laid the grimoire down gently. "Someone go fetch Doirend's book. My spellwork ogham is a bit rusty and I need her lessons to help."

Morgan strode out to get the book and I turned to the others. "Did you selfish sods save me any ice cream?"

Martin grinned and hastily dished me up some mint chocolate chip goodness. As he handed me the bowl, he remarked, "We were going to see if you wanted some but you looked like you were napping when we checked on you. I guess it was a short nap?"

I took the bowl and spooned a mouthful of ice cream in my gob to shut down any emotional reaction. Then I said, "Not a nap, just a small side trip from this wonder." I tapped the grimoire and ate some more mint chocolate chip. The others stared, confused, but I did not elaborate and they didn't press the matter. I finished my ice cream in silence.

Then Morgan returned and any further chance at conversation about what happened dropped away completely.

Morgan thumped the new grimoire down next to Merlin's and I thumbed through the pages until I found the sections on ogham script and spellwork.

"Let's see." I poured over each book, comparing the pages and carefully translating the inscription in Merlin's grimoire with the instructional text from the other book. "All right, the ogham part seems to be an ingredient list, fairly straightforward. I think we have most of what's on the list or can easily obtain it, but this last bit's confusing. It translates as 'strong essence of the kindred of the crimson', not sure what this next part is, maybe, 'aqueduct' or 'river'. I'm not sure what that means."

Morgan peered at it as well and frowned. "Yes, that is

odd. Maybe a variation. Why don't you work on translating the Latin while we gather the rest of the ingredients. Then we'll try and figure out that strange bit."

"Sounds like a plan. Here's what we need: the dried leaf of a rowan, three raven bones, a strip of birch bark, five hawthorn berries, one acorn, a sprig of mistletoe, morning dew, the dust of a woodland faerie's wings, a hair from a seer," I looked at Vivienne, "and one pygmy dragon's claw."

I glanced up at worried faces. "What? I have everything in my travel kit, except the birch bark and the hair. Birch bark shouldn't be too hard to track down and Viv can give up a hair for the cause."

Morgan stared. "What about the pygmy dragon's claw? We can't just find one of those on the nearest street corner."

"Oh, didn't I mention? Just a second." I popped out of the kitchen and retrieved my satchel. I dug the silver box out of a pocket. "A little gift from the Lady." I opened the box and showed off the claw.

"Then what are we waiting for?" Martin jumped to his feet. "I'll nip out and nick a bit of bark. You lot set up the rest of the spell." He dashed off and a few minutes later we heard the door slam.

Martin did love a good spell. "You heard the man. Iseult, go fetch my kit. Vivienne, pluck out a hair and Morgan, you clear off space on that counter while I translate the Latin part of this spell."

Iseult scurried off, Morgan scowled but cleared away the dishes, while Vivienne yanked a strand of hair from her head with a wince. I turned back to the grimoire and wrote out the English version of what we needed to do.

"WELL BLOODY shit!"

Morgan looked up from laying out ingredients at my exclamation. "What? Something wrong?"

"Oh, yes." I massaged my temples, feeling the inklings of a headache forming. "A big something. I've translated the wording and while the spell's powerful, it's an intricate energy working. The damn thing needs to be cast from a location of power. It can't be done here. Plus, I'll need you all as anchors for the spell."

I closed my eyes for a minute. *I'd kill for some whisky.*

Another breath, and I continued, "When we're ready, we'll have to move to a stone circle, a strong ley line, or some other conduit." I looked at the nice row of ingredients Morgan had arranged. "Pack those things up. You'll find a smaller bag in my kit that should work. Sooner or later we're going to have to take this show elsewhere."

I folded the translation of the spell's Latin and tucked it away in my satchel pocket with the box containing the dragon's claw as Morgan organized the ingredients in one of my other bags. As the last of it was ready to travel, Martin arrived back triumphantly holding birch bark.

Morgan plucked it from his hand and added it to the bag. She then handed it to me and I slipped the pack into my satchel.

Martin frowned. "Did I miss something?"

I glanced over at his confused face. "We're going on a road trip. As soon as we figure out this missing ingredient." I tapped Merlin's grimoire.

"Um, okay." He looked at all of us. "Why?"

Morgan answered. "We have to tap into a bigger

power source for the spell. Go full wizard. Merlin loved that shit."

"Oh. So it's not happening right away."

Poor Martin. His expression had turned from excited to confused to crestfallen in minutes. I said, "Cheer up. You'll get to see some ancient power up close. The old magicks are impressive."

That put a grin back on his face, and he chirped, "I'll make some coffee. That'll help us figure out the meaning of that passage. We can go through the books and brainstorm." Martin pranced to the coffee maker and had a nice pot brewing in no time. Then we were all hunkered around the table with steaming cups, pouring over books.

Two hours and four cups of coffee later, I was jumping out of my skin from frustration and caffeine. "The only reference to 'kindred' we found was to striga? And nothing about a crimson river?"

"I did find several bits regarding aqueducts but nothing red about them unless you count a couple of mentions about clay." Martin's expression looked like someone had kicked his dog. There were equally glum faces around the table.

I slammed shut the book I had been reading—*The Willoughby Guide to Archaic Spell Ingredients*—and frowned. "Bollocks to this. Time to get creative."

Morgan looked intrigued. "What did you have in mind?"

"A little unravelling." I gave her my best wicked smile.

Morgan frowned. "Isn't that risky with something like the grimoire?"

"It is," I replied, "but I don't see we have much choice. We can't keep fumbling around in the dark for what we need."

Martin piped up, "What's an unravelling?"

I looked over at him, his whole demeanor waiting expectantly for an answer. "It's like a," I paused, groping for the right words, "a search engine into the past. It probes into a specific written word or phrase—in our case the line in this spell—and unravels the origins. The problem is that it can be tricky to work properly. Plus, I've only used it once and not entirely successfully. If the grimoire decides to fight it, there might be… repercussions."

Martin shook his head. "I'm sure the book won't object. She wants to help. We have to try."

I shot Martin a sharp look, strangely disturbed by his certainty about the grimoire and the familiarity of referring to it as a 'she', but replied, "Yes, we do. It's written down in one of these—"

"I'll do it," Iseult interrupted. I opened my mouth to protest but she held up her hand. "Shush. It's the fastest, best way. I can handle it. I've used the spell with reasonable success and know it well. Even on the grimoire I'm the most capable person to cast it." She took a breath. "Let's get this over with."

I looked at her for a moment. "Okay. Do you need to refresh your memory or do you know it by heart?"

"I'm good, but I'll need a clarity potion."

"I have a prepared one in my kit." I retrieved it and handed it Iseult. She swallowed it.

She inhaled a deep breath and exhaled. "I'm ready. Bring me the grimoire."

I put the book, open to the reversal spell, in front of Iseult. I point to the ogham inscription. "That bit, there."

She nodded and put her fingers over the symbols. "It tingles." Then she closed her eyes and recited the Unravelling.

"From tongues and words, from ink and pen, show me the yesterday, the how and the when. *Implicata, explicare, revelare. Ostende mihi originem.*" The page under her fingers glowed and she stiffened.

"Magic essence and the blood of the kindred. The blood and magic of a witch or wizard, given freely and willingly. Sacrifice for sacrifice. Blood for blood." The words tumbled out of her mouth and then the spell ended. She pulled her hand away from the book and I glimpsed her eyes. They looked haunted. She leaned over and whispered in my ear, and I understood what she saw.

"Well, that seems simple enough. One of us needs to give up some blood." Morgan broke the tension between me and Iseult. "Wouldn't be the first time I drained a bit for some blood magic."

I lowered my gaze. "Yeah, something like that," I lied.

Not so simple, Morgan, not simple at all.

I glanced at Iseult. Her eyes were closed and her hands curled in her lap. I pulled the grimoire away and closed the book, pushing it to the opposite side of the table. "We better tidy up these books and figure out where we're headed."

Iseult shivered as the others began stacking books. The air shifted and I turned. Shadows in the corner swirled and displaced, and a familiar figure appeared.

"Shit! That shadow creature is here! And if he's here, then maybe..." My words choked off in my throat as she walked into the kitchen.

I curled my lip in distaste as snarls, gasps and whimpers sounded from the others.

"Hello, Morgawse."

Chapter Twenty-Four

Morgawse Returns

She stood there without a word, while the shadow creature shuffled and lurked behind her. The scene reminded me of a loyal dog and master. I moved a step closer to Merlin's grimoire. Her eyes gazed towards the book.

"Found the solution to save the world yet?" She tilted her chin and smirked.

"Why are you here?" I slid between her and the grimoire. "Doing more of Nostradamus' dirty work, or working for someone else?"

"Fuck them all, I'm here for the book. With it I'll not be beholden or enslaved to anyone." She shifted position.

"Branching out on your own, then? I can see wanting

to free yourself from Nostradamus, but what about the wizard in the shadows?" I nodded at the creature. "I wager your pet's master won't be happy with you stealing the book."

"He's no pet!" Morgawse snarled. Apparently I hit a nerve. "As for that wizard and his schemes, he can go to hell. What he's done... well I'll take my revenge with that book. Hand it over."

I inched closer to the table. I noticed Morgan moved a few steps sideways and a sliver of magic slid along Iseult's hand.

"You're forgetting one thing."

"What?" She smirked. "That you will all try to stop me? I'm prepared to fight."

"No. You're forgetting the grimoire doesn't like you."

I placed my hand on the book and channelled its power for one quick down and dirty burst of magic that I slammed straight into Morgawse. The barrage hit her square in the gut, propelling her backward into her shadow pet. She screamed, it shrieked, and they both careened into the kitchen wall. Morgan and Iseult followed up with more magical attacks leaving her a moaning heap on the floor. A few seconds later she was silent.

The shadow creature did not go down so easily.

It slithered and swirled, both murk and substance, somehow shifting between mist and matter; its fists rained blows against us in a furious attack, while our magic sailed through its body to no effect. The kitchen became a battleground, magic ripping apart furniture and gouging divots in walls. Curses and screams bounced around the room along with a lot of flying crockery.

I banged up against an unconscious Morgawse, clueless on how to stop the rampaging shadow. Then it hit me, or rather I had hit her. The solution was Morgawse herself.

I grabbed Morgawse by the hair and shouted. "Shadow creep! Back it the hell off, or the witch gets it!" I held my fingers like a gun to her temple, sparks of magic sizzling around my skin. "I'll fry her brain like an egg."

I captured all the creature's attention. It stopped attacking and stared at me with its dark blank face. Even without features, I felt the rage rolling off it.

"So you do care." It heaved, like breathing, its inky mist coiling inward around its body. "I don't want to hurt her but I will if you force me. Just disappear and she stays in one piece."

The creature hovered, as if contemplating, then behind it a shimmer of portal energy materialized. It stepped through, the magic closed around it, and it vanished.

"Well, that was way too easy." I dropped Morgawse, who thumped back to the floor. I made a dash for the kitchen table and snatched up the grimoire. I looked around for my satchel and noticed it by the doorway.

"Yeah," Morgan agreed. I glanced over, and watched her wave a bottle of vodka. Leave it to her to suss out the booze. "That thing will be back for her." She took down some glasses and poured out some alcohol for everyone. "Speaking of which, what are we going to do with her?"

To which Vivienne, of all people, replied, "I packed those binding shackles."

I did a double take. "You what?"

She shrugged. "I had a feeling we'd need them." She turned to Morgan. "Make mine double vodka please while I retrieve them." She skipped off, and I mean literally skipped, humming a tune while Morgan poured out more liquor. I grabbed my glass and plopped my arse down in a chair. Iseult and Martin took theirs in turn but remained standing.

Morgan simply leaned on the countertop swirling her vodka around in the glass.

"So we're just going to sit here all morose in the shambles of the kitchen?" I downed my shot in one gulp. The burn of the alcohol felt good.

An all-around chorus of 'yes' answered me. I shrugged, then got up and poured another drink. "Not good enough. We need to truss up little Miss Betrayal Witch over there and high-tail it out of here with her in tow."

Morgan looked over with a stony glare. "What? Shouldn't we confine her? I know we don't have time for stasis, but dragging her along is courting trouble."

I shook my head. "She's insurance. And she might talk to save bits of her hide. I'm through playing a defensive game. Time to get mean."

I finished my vodka and nodded at Martin. "There a car attached to this place?"

"Yes. I asked to borrow my mate's." Martin swallowed hard. "We're not going to wreck it though, are we? I'm going to have a hard enough time explaining the state of this kitchen."

"Don't worry about that. The kitchen we can fix afterwards, the car too if it comes to that. But we need to keep on the move."

Martin didn't look convinced but Vivienne returned at that moment and ended the conversation. I slapped the shackles on Morgawse and after Vivienne swallowed her drink, we bundled ourselves and some necessities into the car, and hit the road.

SOMEWHERE AFTER midnight we were well into the rural countryside of Surrey and holed up at some empty cottage set back from a winding country road. Martin was snivelling a bit about breaking and entering and ending up in jail, but everyone else flopped down somewhere for some sleep. I dragged a now conscious and cursing Morgawse upstairs for a private chat.

I shoved her in a dusty bedroom and into a ratty old chair. More dust floated upward making her cough. I waited until the chest spasms stopped, then started in on her.

"Spill it, Morgawse, everything you know."

She sneered. "Why should I? I don't give a shit about your little valiant do-gooders and whatever quest you're wound up over. I got sidelined for centuries in hibernation limbo by you and my sister. If some madman of a wizard hadn't kidnapped me into this mess, I'd still be there. I'd rather see you all rot than help you."

"I know that." It was my turn to sneer. "Did you think I'd forgotten how selfish you are, how incapable of taking responsibility for your own actions? I don't expect your help, Morgawse. I expect you to tell me everything you know about what's going on to save yourself some pain. Because if you don't tell me what you know I will rearrange your insides. And I can tell you from personal experience it is quite excruciating to have your liver and your lungs exchange places."

I had the immense satisfaction of seeing her eyes flicker in fear. "You wouldn't." She tried to bluff past my threat with a bit of bravado.

I pulled up another chair and sat down inches from her. "You know me better than that. You know I'm quite willing to hurt you. I'm tired of all the selfish shit that comes my way from fools like you that think magic is all about control. Merlin, the Fisher King, Mark, Tristan, Elaine, you. And you infect and hurt other people. Good people like Nostradamus, Percival, Lancelot, Iseult, even your own son, Mordred." His name sent a ripple of emotion seething across her face. "You regret that one don't, you? Everything that led up to his ending."

With a hiss, she snapped a strained look at me. "What do you know about that? You know nothing about my pain." She bit her lip and stopped talking.

"I know more than you realize. There are a few other forces at play. They let some secrets out of the bag."

"They should have minded their own business."

"I tend to agree with you, but they seem to have a need to meddle. What I want to know is, why is your son important?"

"He's not. He's a victim. No one cares about him except me. It's the bastard that destroyed him, turned him into..." She clenched her jaw. "That's who's messing with magic. That bastard hurt Mordred for his own amusement and now he's back."

Surprise unexpectedly made me shiver. "I thought you banished him to some hell of a netherworld?"

"I did. I don't know... he escaped somehow. He changed into some ruined form of his previous self, but I know it's him. It has to be." She tilted her head up, defiant. "That's why I wanted the grimoire. To bring back my son. And turn that wizard's precious plans to ash."

I huffed. "Apparently everybody wants that job but me."

"Yet, here you are." Morgawse cocked her head. "Why don't you go home and let me handle it?"

I snorted. "I can't do that. I got appointed against my will by the same forces that spilled your secrets."

"So we both have bastards pulling strings and using us as pawns in some game." She chuckled. "They don't know us well, do they?"

I grinned. "No. They don't."

"This doesn't change anything, though. Me telling you things. I'll still try to escape, still try to take the grimoire."

"I know." A hint of regret glided around my brain. "Do you know anything more about this wizard's grand plan? There must be more to this than destruction and anarchy."

"From what…" she oddly hesitated before continuing, "I learned, this wizard wants control." She licked her lips. "It's elegant, really. He set up a chain reaction of tainted magic, entwined with his own cursed essence. The more it spreads and corrupts, the more he controls the underlying structure of magic. What it stains becomes his, until he controls everything. No one will be able to work magic unless he wills it."

"Fuck!" I ground my teeth. "Another fucking despot. Any idea what he'll do if he gets that powerful?"

She shrugged. "I have no idea what his endgame is. Maybe he wants to rule the world."

"Not if I can stop him." I rose from the chair. "Make yourself comfortable. You should try to get some sleep."

I stepped back, summoning a touch of energy and spoke, "*Rhwch eirchar dynnar charam imyanc.*" Strands of magic wrapped around her and bound her to the chair.

She snarled. "You bitch."

"What, you thought I'd let you wander around without safeguards tonight? Shackles or no, you're staying put while I get some shuteye." I flicked my fingers and a gag of energy slapped itself over her mouth. "Don't want you screeching like a banshee all night."

I let her fume, wandered over to bed and laid down. I closed my eyes and drifted off to sleep.

I STOOD inside a house, not the place where we took refuge but an older home in a different time. A fire burned in a hearth, and a long wooden table dominated the room. Glass vials, beakers, jars and earthenware bowls littered the tabletop. Preserved specimens of animal parts and books lined the shelves built into the walls. I recognized the decor, if not the specific place.

"I'm in a wizard's sanctum." My voice echoed as if through a tin pot. "And I'm fucking dreamwalking."

I moved around the table to the books on the shelf, examining the titles. *Seraphim's Blood Magic, Forbidden Alchemy and Magic, Horace's Guide to Dark Spirits and Possession*, and many more titles concerning the dark occult practices. The specimen jars held preserved bat wings, dead toads, lizard scales, faerie wings, and what looked like a unicorn horn. I also saw deadly nightshade, wolfsbane, hemlock, yew, and nettle. All main ingredients of nefarious spells.

I mused aloud, "A dark wizard's home. Maybe *the* dark wizard?" The sound of footsteps caused me to move back, slinking off into the shadows. I watched a tall man enter the room, with long, black hair and a scar slicing across his cheek. I didn't recognize him, but behind him trailed a younger man that I did know. Mordred.

They moved to the table, staring down at a sheet of parchment. The man addressed Mordred, "This is the spell. It will enhance your power, make you stronger. That is what you wanted, correct? Something to make you a more formidable wizard?" The man rubbed his hands together and something about the gesture made me shiver.

Mordred, however, was oblivious. He eagerly snatched the spell to study it and his face lit up in joy. "Yes, thank you. Thank you."

I moved out from the shadows and held my breath. No one reacted. As with the memories, I was a ghost. I shifted behind Mordred, and read the spell over his shoulder. On the surface, the words seemed right, but I couldn't shake the feeling of something being off.

I turned towards the other man, "What are you up to? I won't…" The words died in my throat as I realized I could do nothing. Whatever happened, it was over ages ago.

I turned back to study the spell. The more I read, the more my skin prickled at the double-edged wording. The veneer of it read like but an enhancement spell, but… then it clicked.

"Shit! You bastard! This won't enhance his magic. It's a fundamental conduit spell of some sort. But for what?" I scowled at the wizard. "You disguised the real intent brilliantly, I'll give you that. I'm not surprised Mordred was fooled. Especially if he trusted you." I looked at Mordred with pity. "You always trusted the wrong people. Like Cwyllog and her father."

I shifted position as Mordred placed the parchment back on the table. He and the wizard moved off, discussing something in hushed tones. I didn't listen, focusing all my attention towards the spell.

"Why were you trying to fool Mordred? This bit looks like a syncing of magical harmonies, as if you were working a tandem spell, but then it shifts as if…" A horrid thought suddenly occurred to me and I glanced over at Mordred and the man who was not his friend. "You *are* the one who drained his magic and stole his soul. But by the look of it, this spell does more than that. It would leave the victim… Shit!"

Everything clicked. Morgawse, the shadow creature, their attachment. "That poor beast is all that's left of Mordred. Nothing but a puppet essence of his soul, his immortality. Bound to this fucking wizard forever." I recoiled in disgust and horror and the room faded away.

I opened my eyes to see the morning sunlight streaming in the window of the bedroom. I glanced over at Morgawse. She was napping in her chair, still trussed up like a holiday turkey. I stared at the ceiling, letting what had happened to Mordred bounce around in my brain. I never liked the young man but he did not deserve that fate. A simmering, white hot anger grew deep within me. I'd end that bastard of a dark wizard at all costs.

Morgawse stirred and I glanced over. She opened her eyes and the words came out of my mouth without a thought.

"Mordred is that shadow creature, isn't he? That's why you're working with him. You're still trying to save him."

I watched the muscles in her jaw twitch. "Figured it out, did you? Goody. And yes, I'm going to save him, restore what he was. I sent him there, to that man. It's my fault."

I remained silent. I didn't have the heart to tell what she wanted was probably impossible. Mordred's magic had most likely been absorbed by the wizard. His spirit was corrupted and bound. To break that curse and restore his soul into his body… well, it would take more magic than Morgawse possessed, even if she had the grimoire. Restoring his soul might kill him and breaking the bond between the wizard and Mordred would destroy his immortality. Mordred would never be a wizard again.

Fuck that wizard. He wouldn't get away with it. Not any of it. He's trying to suck the heart out of magic the same way…

Then it dawned on me. His endgame. I scrambled off the bed and headed for the door. I left the bedroom with Morgawse's voice shouting, "I will save Mordred! The grimoire is mine!" in my wake.

I rushed down the stairs, my feet thumping a

thunderous beat at each step, and dashed into the main sitting room. Morgan and Vivienne were snoozing on a sofa and in an armchair respectively. Iseult and Martin were elsewhere.

I yelled, "Wake up!" and they jolted out of their slumber. "Get your things and get to the car. Now!" Then I sprinted off to find the other two.

I found Martin in a downstairs bedroom and Iseult asleep upstairs. I shook them both awake and told them to pack up and head out to the car. Then I collected my own things and dragged Morgawse downstairs and out of the cottage.

I bundled us into the car where the others were waiting.

Morgan snapped, "Why the rush? We didn't even have breakfast."

"No more delays. I'm sick of power-hungry bastards hurting people. We're going to fuck up that dark wizard and blow his grand scheme back to hell!" I ground my teeth as Morgan started up the car, pulling out of the driveway and onto the road. "And then I'm going to tell the damn Lady to go to hell too. If she had just explained everything from the damn beginning we'd be out ahead of this mess."

"So where are we headed?" I heard Martin's slightly scared voice from the back seat.

"Stonehenge. The only place strong enough to undo this looming disaster."

As Morgan sped up the car, I heard Morgawse's mocking laughter.

Chapter Twenty-Five

Nostradamus Returns

An hour and a half later we were in sight of Salisbury Plain, after a quick detour for a takeout breakfast to silence the complaints and rumbling stomachs. The morning sun glinted down from a blue sky and for once I felt optimistic.

I should have known it wouldn't last.

A great bolt of lightning and fire rained down from the sky and struck the road in front of us, a lurking figure striding out of the smoke. Morgan fought to keep the car out of the ditch, swerving around the figure like mad, with the tail end swinging us about like a top. We skidded to a stop, pointed in the opposite direction, but still on the road.

I stared out the windscreen as an angry Nostradamus

stalked towards us, magic sparking all around him.

"Bloody hell! Can't that man stay imprisoned and out of my hair until I need him?"

I yanked the handle and pushed open the car door, blasting out at a dead run and racing to the front of the auto. I slid an energy ball straight down the middle of the road and knocked the blighter off his feet. He tumbled along the roadway and into the crash barrier. Momentarily distracted by Morgan and Iseult jumping out of the car, I turned, and during my lack of attention Nostradamus scrambled to his feet.

He screamed, "*Ente pête, patiz,*" and a wild gust of wind sent us toppling onto our arses. As I clambered to my feet, he uttered another spell and the car levitated into the air, spinning and turning on its side. The doors flung themselves open and Martin, Morgawse, and Vivienne plummeted to the road, followed by most of our baggage. The car sailed on, before it landed gracefully back on four tyres halfway down a hillside.

I watched everything and everyone scatter with my satchel and the grimoire bouncing along the pavement. I raced to retrieve both. I grabbed the leather strap of my bag, hoisting it on my shoulder, but Nostradamus got to the grimoire first.

He seized it with a smirk and a yelp, wrapping it in the folds of his jacket and taking off at a full run down the road. I lit out after him, bashing through our scattered belongings, with at least two people chasing me. I didn't look back to see who, just ran full tilt at the thorn in my side stealing the grimoire. When a portal opened in front of him, I ran faster.

Nostradamus barrelled through the magic gateway, but by then I was on his heels and jumped in after him. I felt other people slam through the gateway behind me and that's when it all went to hell. The presence of that many people overloaded the magic, and we careened out of control. I caught glimpses of Morgan and Morgawse as we roller-coasted through dimensions.

I reached out in desperation as we continually bashed about in the runaway portal and caught the edge of the magic. A few whispered words and I shifted the chaotic ride right where we needed to be: smack dab in the middle of Stonehenge.

I looked up, expecting to see the shocked faces of tourists or site workers gaping at us, but somehow we had landed during a lull or maybe it was just too early. Either way, we got lucky and no one witnessed us fall from a hole in the sky. Only the birds and the clouds greeted our arrival.

I counted heads as we all dusted ourselves off: Besides myself, Nostradamus, Morgan and Morgawse stood within the confines of the stones. No one else had followed us in. Nostradamus still held the grimoire which fought his grip and I noticed Morgawse had lost her shackles.

"Morgawse!" My shout cracked the tension and she nearly jumped out of her skin. "How did you free yourself?"

She laughed nervously, almost maniacally, and shouted back, "You can thank him." She waved a hand at Nostradamus. "Banging off the roadway cracked the metal enough to damage an etched rune and snap the spell. Picking the lock was easy after that."

"I'm sure it was." A grunt from Nostradamus interrupted my snide remark and I glared at him. The grimoire danced in his grip, its magic struggling against his clutches. I felt the book's power radiate outward, resonating off the stones surrounding us and the words left my mouth of their own accord.

"Ordd ayer trwr, cerriggal afeich, cym orth."

The ground rumbled and the standing stones flashed in sizzles of electricity, and the ley lines running through Stonehenge surged with energy. The sensation of it coursed through my blood and bone, connecting from the rock and soil into the soles of my feet, from the air to my skin and lungs, filling me with righteous fury and a new reserve of power.

Morgawse took a step backward, smart enough to know what I had done, but Nostradamus sneered.

"More parlour tricks?"

My tongue tasted of metal and rain, of sand and roses. I replied, "No."

Then I upheaved the earth under his feet and tossed him into the air like a rag doll. The grimoire flew from his fingers in a shower of golden sparks sailing to land in front of me with a gentle thump. I slammed Nostradamus back into the earth face first and turned on Morgawse.

"Do you want some?"

She shook her head and made no move to attack or flee. To her right Nostradamus groaned through mouthfuls of grass and dirt. "Then it's time to end all of this."

"*Cyuddi behna aydd lidth wyeld.*"

A glamour rose and encircled Stonehenge. We might be alone but that could change at any moment. Then I turned to Morgawse.

"*Erbynyr arhyiad cerrigyn dalffod.*" She slammed up against a stone, paralysed and safely tucked out of the way. Morgan cleared her throat and I turned my head.

She looked at me with a tinge of fear in her eyes. "What are you doing?"

"What needs to be done. I'm going to bring the others now."

With Stonehenge's power racing through me, I saw the conduits through the netherworlds, the ley lines, and all the ways to access every gateway. I reached out and tracked down the rest of our stalwart group.

"*Ynddi wyni fathyn.*"

I scooped them up from the road in a portal and

slid them through dimensions to land in a surprised heap by Morgan. I heard exclamations and gasps as they slowly realized what had happened. They all turned to me. Vivienne looked at me with something akin to awe and I knew she understood, but the others stared at me with trepidation and dismay. I sympathized, knowing what I must look like to them with this wild magic of ascendant channelling coursing through my body. I probably glowed like a neon sign on a marquee.

However, I had no time for coddling or explanations. I had work to finish and an arsehole wizard to crush.

Chapter Twenty-Six

Dark Wizard

I dug in my satchel and pulled out the bag Morgan had packed earlier and the spell translation, along with my adaptations. I studied the writing for a moment to memorize what must be done. I glanced over at Nostradamus who had passed out.

I stuffed the paper back in my bag and barked orders at the others, "It is essential to begin the spell now. I'll need you to get into place." I marched over and yanked them one by one across the grass to where I needed them to stand, ignoring squeaks of protests and swearing.

I handed each a hawthorn berry, keeping the last one for myself. "Just stand there and hold the berry until

I tell you what to do."

I stepped back and watched them form the proper positions of the circle, with the last place of the ring waiting for me. I sprinkled the dust of the faerie wings at their feet, again saving the final bit for me.

At the centre of this wheel, I formed a triangle with the raven bones and arranged the rowan leaf, the acorn and the birch bark at each outside corner; the sprig of mistletoe went in the middle. I added a touch of magic to hold them all in place and poured the morning dew over the mistletoe.

Then I took my spot, grabbed the hawthorn berry, and dusted the remaining faerie powder on my toes.

"Everyone crush your berry in your hand."

As red juice dripped against our skin, the circle completed itself and the magic snapped into being, crackling an energy ring around and through us. The power surged along our skin and elicited gasps and giggles. I pulled Vivienne's strand of hair from the bag and closed my eyes.

"Invoke five along the circle, to the three of wisdom, and ask the blessing of the earth. Summon the beginning, the protection, the strength. Entreat the sacred life that dawns with the potential of each being, each drop of blood." The ground rumbled and sparks flashed in the air. Then I finished the first part of the spell, "With this token of sight, show me the right path."

Amid our heartbeats, time slowed, the surface of existence freezing like a sheen of ice on a river, while underneath the water of life flowed. I sank into the river below the ice and travelled between the seconds.

I surfaced inside the heart of Stonehenge, the passages to an infinite number of netherworlds stretching out in a complex spider web from the core. A splendour of colours glittered around me in a dazzling spectrum. I gazed in awe at jade and crimson, lemon yellow and caramels, at cobalt hues and amethyst swirling next to indigo. Yet in the midst of the array of tinted grandeur, strands devoid of colour and sparkle threaded their way along the web. To those, I focused my attention.

I stretched out my senses, feeling along the interconnected structure to the cold wretched emptiness that snaked along the darkened threads. I felt the menace, the hollow nothing that engulfed them, the tainted magic that controlled them. I probed their substance, searching for clues, for a way to the source. Deeper, deeper, slashing my way in to see... and then something smashed back, reverberating outward and slamming into my essence with the force of a speeding train.

I screamed, everything about me shaking apart before I pulled it back together and recovered. The air and void around me shivered, shifted, and a purple-black miasma coiled and spiralled, amalgamating into form.

I stared at the astral thing in the shape of a man. "Well now, if it isn't the mysterious Dark Wizard."

"Yes." The word resonated with the force of a booming drum. Then his voice turned raspy, like sound spewed over sandpaper and grit. "I've had other names, but some might call me that. Some, like you, might call me enemy. Yet, I am only being true to who I was born to be, after all the expectations and lies were stripped away." He formed a semblance of a grin. "You know how that truth feels. We both were born of lies and rose above them."

"Is that what this is?" I gestured at the dark threads. "Your truth?"

"Isn't it everyone's? That hidden dingy soul, our pain, all the lies we tell ourselves?" A hiss escaped his lips. "I only released it into our world. To cleanse it bare of foolish notions, of the falsehood that we are more than base, selfish creatures. Magic was born to fulfill that promise of darkness and I was born to create the perfect world."

I snorted. "Bollocks! You're still full of lies. You don't want to cleanse the world, you just want to control it, create a chain reaction. When magic implodes, you'll be there to channel it. You used that poor nymph as a conduit to reroute the heart of magic to you. You want to absorb its power and become some sort of god. You're after Ascendancy without restrictions or risk. Same as Nostradamus only on a bigger scale." I stepped closer, my hands clenched and my chin raised. "Admit it."

He tilted his head up and laughed. "What if I am? Everyone needs a hobby. Your French lover had the right idea, wrong ambition. I won't just be a god, I'll be *the* god. The God of Magic. And I'll be free."

"Oh, please, you're just a tosser with a complex." I snorted my derision. "Whatever you're after, it isn't going to happen."

"So you are here to stop me. At the behest of the Lady."

I sneered. "Fuck the Lady. I'm here just to kick your vainglorious arse."

"I'd like to see you try!" His shadows spat little fizzing tendrils. Then he added, "At least we hold *her* in the same contempt. Maybe you did learn your lesson from Merlin." He chuckled. "But even so, you're on her side. The wrong side."

I narrowed my eyes and scowled. Whoever he was, he knew things. I filed that tidbit away in my head for later. "I told you, I'm not here for her. I'm doing this for me."

I closed my eyes and took a deep breath, feeling the primal nature of this nexus. My next words sang from the depths of my soul directly to the heart of magic.

"I walk with the earth, I soar along the wind, I drown in the water, I survive past the fire, and I beseech you. Stand against the dark. Hold against the dark."

This veiled beast of man screamed and I opened my eyes to see strands of magic slashing, slithering, wrapping around his body, imprisoning his form and power. And all around me a wall of energy grew, keeping the dark corruption at bay.

"That won't hold you forever, but long enough to finish what must be done."

He spat at me and shouted, "You haven't the courage to finish this, to offer what must be given to reverse my spell. You'll fail!"

I laughed, a hollow cold sound. "You don't know me at all, if you believe that."

I looked beyond him then, as he struggled, and glimpsed the image of the Lady, her figure wavering along a thread of blue light. I flipped her off and returned to my flesh and bone.

Expectant faces stared at me. The circle of magic faded to a faint glow. "The first part is done, but we haven't much time to reverse the blood sacrifice. Everyone remain in place, no matter what happens. Understand?"

They all nodded, avoiding looking at me directly. My gaze drifted towards Nostradamus. My stomach knotted as I moved, walking over to his side. A slap against his face and a jolt of magic brought him back to the land of the wakeful. He rolled onto his back, his eyes full of confusion.

"What have you done?"

"What you wanted. I'm saving magic." I touched his cheek gently, letting him feel the connection to Stonehenge. "But I'm sorry, old friend. It's time to fulfil your final prophecy. It is time for you to end."

Chapter Twenty-Seven

Casting the Spell

"*Non! Non!*" He snarled and sat up, pushing me away with a flurry of French curses. I slapped him again, hard. Four other faces stared at us, but no one said a word. I could feel their fear as well as his. I softened my expression and tried to soothe him.

"Sometimes fate is fate, Michel. Accept it. But the choice must be yours. The spell says blood and magic given freely and willingly."

"Of course it does. Why must it be me?" He stared at the ground and whispered, "Perhaps it is all wrong, my vision. Perhaps…" His words trailed off as I shook my head.

"If you do this you will be gone. No longer flesh

and blood. Your essence will be bound in the spell, like the nymph, caught in its threads for eternity. But you may become something else, something more."

A sheen of tears trembled at the edge of his eyes and his lips quivered. "I do not want that. I do not want to die. You were right. Magic was an escape for me. An escape from death. How can I do this?"

I stroked his cheek, part of me feeling shitty for what I was about to do and say. "This isn't a death, Michel. We're just creating a new type of Ascension. You won't die, not buried in the cold ground, and your essence won't be scattered across the matrix." I kept my voice calm, to reassure him. "Yes, you will not be this person, but that's because you will transcend. I'm going to bind you within the heart of Stonehenge, forever flowing within the rivers of magic, always and eternally its guardian."

I stroked his cheek again, like I would a frightened child. "Think of the knowledge that will unfold before you, what wonders you will see. You will *be* magic, Michel. Forever and always." I smiled at him like I used to back in France. "That won't be so bad a fate."

He stared at me, brushing his fingers against a strand of my hair. "There was never any fighting this, was there? I was brought to you so I would do this thing. For if I don't, you will. Won't you?"

I nodded and held my breath. I wondered if he would trade his life for mine.

He straightened his shoulders. "*C'est la vie.* What do you need me to do?"

I whispered words in his ear, then rose and helped Michel to his feet. "Come stand in the centre of our circle." I led him to where he needed to be and he knelt beside the top point of the triangle of raven bones. I reached into my bag, pulled out my pocket knife and handed it to him. "Spill your blood over the bones. I'll do the rest."

I watched him cut his thumb and drip the blood over the three bones of a raven. When he finished staining the bones, he handed me the knife. He sat back on his heels, folded his hands in his lap and the circle flared back into full power. We looked at each other—he with an aspect of acceptance on his face—and he nodded.

Michel murmured, "*Lier,*" and I felt his magic connect

with Stonehenge. He lifted his head towards the sky.

I slit open his throat.

A chorus of shouts and gasps reverberated across the circle, but no one moved from their position. I held Nostradamus' head over the bones and let his blood gush across them and soak into the earth. Then I laid his body down gently beside the spellwork, and whispered, "*Rhwym wchyn.*" A flash of energy reached up and tethered his flesh to the spell. I dropped the knife. With trembling fingers, I fished out the dragon claw from my bag and dipped it into his blood.

Clenching my jaw against the screams welling in my throat, I moved away and took my place at the edge of the circle. As I readied myself, I caught sight of the growing bloodstains on Michel's clothing and it took everything I had not to collapse in tears. Then I cut into the heel of my palm with the claw. A surge of power shot through me—the raw energy of dragon essence—and I felt the connection to Michel's magic through our mingled blood.

My voice shook as I recited the last of the spell, "From the kindred we seek balance, from the blood we seek life, from the magic we bring renewal." Magic flared around the circle again, lighting it in a golden glow. In the centre, the raven bones glowed green and Michel's body shuddered.

A crack of energy shook the air and suddenly the disembodied voice of Nostradamus resonated from inside the circle. "I feel it. I feel it all. The power, the corruption. It is so much more, so much more than I imagined or realized."

I clenched my jaw and blocked out his voice, closing my eyes to the world around me. I chanted, "Take the gift offered freely, kindred blood, kindred magic. Cleanse the heart, reweave the threads, make whole what has been torn."

He screamed and I opened my eyes.

Flames of gold and green engulfed Michel, consuming his flesh and bones, transforming any mortal part of him, draining him, absorbing him into the heart of Stonehenge. I felt tears on my cheeks as I watched the man I knew disappear into something new, something living in pure visceral magic. I said the last of the spell without a goodbye.

"Into the earth I cast you, to the long road I entrust you, I will see you on your way in farewell and fate."

A flash of raw ancient magic erupted from the

standing stones, passing through all our bones, and we all came through the fire into the world beyond. The transformed Nostradamus stood tall; a shining beacon of magical energy. He stepped beyond the circle and the beating heart of Stonehenge embraced him. With not even a glance backward, he vanished. The astral forms of Vivienne, Morgan, Iseult and Martin returned to the physical world, leaving me alone.

Until he arrived.

The Dark Wizard, the would-be god king. He limped, if such a thing could be possible on this plane, and his form seemed broken and weakened. As Nostradamus did his work, as the web of threads brightened and the darkness died piece by piece, the wizard faded, snarling and screaming as he fought to maintain control.

He turned his angry focus to me. "You could have had everything if you had joined me. We could have ruled together. Why would you save it? Destroy the majesty that could have been?"

I didn't answer. I only stared at him with pity.

He continued to rant, spewing venom at me. "How could you? Why would you side with them? The ones who manipulate and move us like pawns? You were as much a victim as me! I know you hate what you are. I offered you the chance to have revenge, to burn it all to the ground! Why didn't you take it?"

I curled my lip. "You offered me nothing but another lie."

"And you think the Lady offers you truth?" He winced, his body shuddering.

I shook my head. "I don't want what she's offering either. I told you. I didn't do it for her. Or anyone else. The decision I made was for me."

I saw the hate in his dark eyes. "You haven't won." He doubled over in pain and then snarled at me like a cornered animal. "I'll just find someone else. Another fool willing to sacrifice themselves. Cast the spell over again. You won't stop it next time."

"There will be no next time." I watched his shadowy face twist in pain and confusion. "That's the reason I chose Stonehenge. The reason I wanted Nostradamus to be the sacrifice." I looked around at the growing power. "Can't you see what's happening? He's here, he's part of the heart now, flowing along the ley lines, the threads, touching every part of the cosmic interlace of power. He knows how to control it, how to be an eternal guardian to the wild energy that flows here. He'll protect against your darkness, or any threat that seeks to harm the fabric of magic. Your spell or any similar spell is useless now."

With a howl of rage, the wizard vanished. I lingered, watching the remnant of Michel continue to repel the dark magic and repair the damage. Part of me wanted to say something, tell him all the things I never said in life, but I knew it was pointless. He couldn't hear me, and probably wouldn't even recognize me anymore. Anything of his mortal existence had been wiped away.

I sighed and faded back to my life, leaving him to his new one.

As I came back to my reality, the last of Stonehenge's magic left me, siphoning back into the standing stones. I had an empty hollow feeling in my gut and I wanted to close my eyes and wish the world away. Morgan's voice asked, "Is it done? Is it over? Are we safe?"

"Yes." I stared down at my hands, seeing the dried

blood stains on my palms.

His blood on my hands.

"Can we go home now?" Martin's sad voice broke through my self-pity.

Again I replied, "Yes." I dropped the claw into my bag and walked over to the leavings of the spell. I bent down, scooped the blood-stained knife, bones and plants into my bag as well, and stood back up. I smushed any remaining traces into the grass and dirt with my foot, then took a vial of portal dust out of my satchel.

"Let's go home." I tossed a handful of dust and opened a portal back to my cottage. Iseult, Martin and Vivienne all hurried through, without a word or a glance towards me. Morgan hesitated for a minute, as if wanting to speak, then turned her head away and stepped through the gateway.

I took one last look around, hoping for a sense of him, but all I felt was the wind on my face. I also noticed Morgawse was gone, but I didn't care. I stepped through the portal releasing the glamour as I left, letting the illusion of normal reality continue.

Chapter Twenty-Eight

Regrets

After our return, Iseult and Vivienne fled upstairs, Vivienne with a bottle of wine and Iseult with a box of chocolates snitched from my pantry. I didn't blame either of them for isolating themselves in their bedrooms after what had happened. After what I did. Michel's face was haunting my thoughts. I kept glancing at my hands expecting to see blood, even after I washed them raw. I felt like fleeing to a mountaintop for a few decades.

I settled for hiding in the garden with a bottle of whisky and a large glass. Within a few minutes of my self-imposed brooding, Morgan joined me with a bottle of red wine, and a full glass.

I glanced over at her. She studied her wine like she was a connoisseur at a tasting. I considered letting the silence remain, but decided to get whatever discussion or confrontation she wanted over.

"Why didn't you head straight back to London?" I sipped some whisky to fortify my courage. "Something on your mind?"

Morgan didn't look at me at first, only drank wine. When she finally did look over at me, it was with sorrow. "You knew before you even started the spell, didn't you? Back in the kitchen. That you'd have to sacrifice someone?"

"I did." I stared into the amber alcohol, swirling it slightly in the glass. "So did Iseult. And I'm fairly sure Vivienne had an inkling too."

"It was still stone cold. What if Nostradamus hadn't stepped up? Would it have been one of us?" Morgan's voice stayed calm, but there was an accusation underneath her words.

"No. I would have done it." I sipped more whisky. "It was how the core of Merlin's spell worked." I glared at the tree. "He set it up so someone had to make a willing sacrifice no matter how you adapted it. But I would have never chosen one of you."

"Easy to say now."

"It is, but it's also the truth." I gulped more whisky, letting it burn down my throat. "And maybe it worked out the way it was meant to be. Michel was the best choice, connected as he was already to the wild magic. Plus, I was fulfilling his own prophecy."

"Still…"

"I know. It was a win for losing and I feel like shit."

"You should." Morgan kicked at the table, rattling the whisky bottle, and topped off her glass of wine. Then she drained it in one gulp and poured another glass. "What you told Nostradamus, to make him agree to sacrifice himself, that was bullshit, wasn't it? The whole thing felt like an Ascension. One you deliberately took too far. Is the bastard even in one piece anymore?"

I shrugged and drowned my guilt in alcohol. "Maybe. Part of what I said was true. He's not a scattered essence; he's still whole in whatever form he became. But I have no idea whether anything of his mind or personality survived, or even if he has a conscious knowledge of anything. He might spend eternity in oblivion, riding the lines of energy as a force of nature guarding the wild magic. I hope what I said was true, but I don't know."

Morgan drank more wine, but stopped talking. Silence sat between us for a long time as the morning faded and the sun moved into afternoon.

Morgan finally broke the tension, asking, "Is he gone then, this other bastard wizard? The one that started this mess?"

I shook my head. "He can't undo the core essence of magic anymore, but he's still out there. I'm sure he's not through causing trouble."

"I wonder who he is?"

"I don't know, but I got the sense we knew him somehow."

"You mean from Camelot? One of us?"

"Maybe. I don't know." I repressed a shudder. "He knew things, spoke with familiarity. He was all shadows and creepiness, so I never saw a face, but I felt like I should know who he was, like we had met before." I leaned my head back. "And at the end, he took his defeat personally, as if I betrayed him somehow."

Any further musings were cut short as Martin bumbled his way into the garden with a plate of sandwiches and holding a bottle of beer. He set the platter down with a clunk on the table and sat down in a chair, after plucking two morsels from the plate. Through greedy bites he said, "I couldn't take being alone in the kitchen anymore. Not after... Well just after everything." He took a swig of beer and another bite of sandwich.

"I don't blame you." Morgan raised her nearly empty glass in a toast and then poured in some more wine from a nearly empty bottle. "It's been a shitty week, and an even more shitty day." She downed a good gulp of wine. "We didn't even get any frequent travel miles for all that portalling."

"I liked that part." Martin's face brightened for a moment. "Seeing all those places. I'd like to visit again, when we're not in a horrible crisis, trying to stop the world from imploding."

I grunted. Morgan just drank. Martin didn't seem to care, for he kept rambling.

"That part wasn't great, all the fights and the dark magic. I didn't like dying at all. And what happened at…" He swallowed more beer. "But things worked out, I guess. Mostly. In the end." Martin took another sandwich and settled back in his chair. "I do wish we'd gotten to visit Millie while we were in Cornwall, though."

I stared for a minute. Sometimes I wondered about Martin. How exactly his mind worked. Daft one minute, insightful the next, and sometimes going off on totally irrelevant tangents.

But we all cope differently, I suppose.

So I only nodded. "Yes. It would have been nice to have had time for a visit."

I sipped whisky, while the wind rustled Merlin's leaves. Off in the distance I watched the shadows shift and tried not to shiver. Then the three of us sat there, in the garden, and watched the sunset. I let the whisky soften my mood and relaxed.

Somewhere from the ether a voice whispered in my ear, "You can't escape fate."

I gripped my glass, waiting for the others to

react. Nothing.

Just for me then?

I sipped my whisky. My fingers clenched the arm of my chair, and I mustered as much bravado as I could manage.

Bring it on you wankers. Fuck you. And fuck fate.

I felt the wind brush against my face, but no answering voice. The shadows deepened in the garden and the light faded on the day.

IF YOU enjoyed these adventures of Nimue and her friends, and would like to know more, sign up for my newsletter at my website (https://afstewart.ca/) for the latest news on the Camelot Immortals series. And be sure to check out the prequel short stories in Eternal Myths, to read what happened with Merlin and how Elaine and Martin went after the Grail.

What to expect in upcoming books.

Gathering Hallows: The Camelot Immortals Book Two
Running from the consequences of her actions, Nimue

takes off on a series of adventures that lead back to a quest for the Hallows of Britain.

Broken Branch: The Camelot Immortals Book Three
Old friends and foes resurface, secrets are revealed, and the identity of the Dark Wizard is exposed. Plus, Nimue goes to therapy.

Wayward Prophecy: The Camelot Immortals Book Four
Nimue faces her destiny in an all out magical war.

THANK YOU for reading this book. If you enjoyed it, please consider taking the time to leave an honest review. Authors appreciate reader feedback.

If you'd like to know more about me or my books, please drop me a line at my website, Welcome to Avalon.

A. F. STEWART was born and raised in Nova Scotia, Canada, and still calls it home. The youngest in a family of seven children, she is a steadfast and proud sci-fi and fantasy geek with an overly creative mind and an active imagination. She favours the dark and deadly when writing—her genres of choice being dark fantasy and horror—but she has been known to venture into the light on occasion. As an indie author, she's published novels, novellas and story collections, with a few side trips into poetry.

MORE BOOKS BY A. F. STEWART

Poetry:

Horror Haiku and Other Poems

Horror Haiku Pas de Deux

Places of Poetry

Colours of Poetry

Reflections of Poetry

Shadows of Poetry

Tears of Poetry

Multi-Author Anthologies:

Cogs, Crowns, and Carriages

Hell's Empire: Tales of the Incursion

Abandon: 13 Tales of Impulse, Betrayal, Surrender, and Withdrawal

A Twist of Fate: A Collection of 11 Twisted Fairy Tales

Beyond the Wail

Legends and Lore

Mechanized Masterpieces

Christmas Lites Series (Books III-IX)

Coffin Hop: Death by Drive-In

Fiction:

Eternal Myths

Ghosts of the Sea Moon (Saga of the Outer Islands Book I)

Souls of the Dark Sea (Saga of the Outer Islands Book II)

Renegades of the Lost Sea (Saga of the Outer Islands Book III)

Chronicles of the Undead

Killers and Demons

Killers and Demons II: They Return

Fairy Tale Fusion

Gothic Cavalcade

Ruined City